SLICK SENATOR

A Cocky Hero Club Story

MIKA LANE

JOIN MY INSIDER GROUP

Stay in the know
Join my Insider Group
Exclusive access to private release specials, giveaways,
the opportunity to receive advance reader copies
(ARCs), and other random musings.

Let's keep in touch
Mika Lane Newsletter
Email me
Visit me! www.mikalane.com
Friend me! Facebook
Pin me! Pinterest
Follow me! Twitter
Laugh with me! Instagram

COPYRIGHT

Slick Senator is a standalone story inspired by Vi Keeland and Penelope Ward's *British Bedmate*. It's published as part of the Cocky Hero Club world, a series of original works, written by various authors, and inspired by Keeland and Ward's *New York Times* bestselling series.

Want to keep up with all of the new releases in Vi Keeland and Penelope Ward's Cocky Hero Club world? Make sure you sign up for the official Cocky Hero Club newsletter for all the latest on our upcoming books: https://www.subscribepage.com/CockyHeroClub Check out other books in the Cocky Hero Club series: http://ww.cockyheroclub.com

ISBN print 978-1-948369-36-7

Like deals and other cool stuff?
Sign up for the Mika Lane newsletter!

CHAPTER ONE

CRICKET

I t had been an excellent week for death.

Which was awesome.

At least, for me.

Maybe not so much for the folks who'd passed into the great beyond. Rest in peace, and all that.

But it was guaranteed employment for the obituary writers of the world.

Yes, indeed. I worked at the internationally renowned Washington Chronicle, where I was a decidedly not-renowned obituary writer. And if that weren't dreary enough, I sat in the gloomy corner of our open-plan office, in a cube that was once—and still was—used for the corpses of dead office equipment and other crap that had served its useful life at the newspaper. Kind of appropriate for the obits department.

In one corner was a stack of precariously balanced computer monitors that had either conked out or been rendered obsolete. On the other side was a box of busted staplers and three-ring binders. At my feet were half-used legal pads and spiral notebooks that folks hadn't quite used up—but didn't quite want to toss out, either.

Every now and then, I'd grab our mail cart and drag as much of the crap to the dumpster as possible.

And like spawn, it piled up again, my coworkers apparently untrainable.

As I was getting settled in to another day of ignoring my nasty surroundings, something rustled behind me.

I turned to see my boss. "Oh hey, Wayne, how's your day going?"

"Hey, Cricket," he said, hitching up his high waters even higher and avoiding my eyes, "I guess you saw we got a bunch of orders this morning."

Orders. That's what Wayne called requests for obits. They usually came from our editor in chief and others who attended the weekly editorial meeting.

Which did not include me.

I nodded, wishing for once, Wayne would look me in the eye instead of acting like I had girl cooties.

"I did see that. I'm already jamming on—" I sifted through a pile of folders on my desk, "—that guy who invented the digital fishing lure."

That was going to be a doozy.

Writing obits was not a bad job, truth be told. I described it as being a lot like churning out mini-history lessons. I'd do some research, interview some people, and construct a one-thousand-word story about the life of the deceased—of course, always positive and joyous. They were a celebration, not a sad goodbye, Wayne liked to remind me.

He glanced at my boobs and looked away quickly, his face beet red. And I pretended I'd seen nothing. Just like I always did.

It's not anyone who could be an obits editor for their entire career, but it sure suited my painfully awkward boss. He loved nothing more than hunkering down in front of his computer and banging out obit after obit, so cleanly written that the proofreaders and the legal department rarely had to make any changes.

Seriously, it was the perfect job for Wayne.

Not so much for me.

"Seems like you've got it under control, Cricket. Cool. *Tres* cool."

Did people still say *tres cool?*

He slithered back to his cube, which, lucky for me, was on the other side of the sprawling office known as the *newsroom*.

I could usually plow through my work, leaving myself free time to surf the net and look at puppy videos. But Christ, a lot of people had died over the weekend, creating a shit ton of work for me. And wouldn't you know, not a single one of them was somebody we were ready for.

It was common practice to have pre-written obits for the most famous folks, especially really old ones like Queen Elizabeth and Keith Richards—people who could go at any moment. We kept those carefully researched and written masterpieces on ice, so to speak, in preparation for the day those people passed. The Washington Chronicle would not be caught with its pants down. We were ready.

And when one of those folks did depart our world, we simply pulled their obit out of the files and dusted it off to see if it needed a little sprucing up. Those were the easy days. We were ahead of the game.

Not so much today.

So, I did what I always did when faced with an overwhelming amount of work. I Googled *cute puppies*.

I was obsessed with puppies. I wanted one so badly I could taste it. But the crappy apartment I lived in didn't permit them because, god forbid, a dog might make it even more crappy than it already was.

So, until I lived in a place that welcomed four-legged fur babies, I was forced to satisfy my longing at DogHouse, the local shelter for rescues, where I volunteered to play with and walk dogs several times a week.

"Hey."

Shit.

I was so startled by my next visitor that I knocked over my cup of coffee, which spilled all over the dead computer monitors next to my desk. I quickly switched screens on my computer, hoping whoever had sneaked up behind me hadn't seen me watching YouTube videos of the five basic commands every puppy should be taught.

Aimee, my work BFF, propped her butt on the corner of my desk, causing a messy pile of papers to flutter to the floor.

There was nowhere else to sit.

"You scared the crap out of me."

"Why are you so jumpy?" she asked, snooping through the papers on my desk. "You cruising porn again?" Her blue eyes twinkled wickedly.

She was by far the coolest person I worked with.

I peered around the corner of my cube and lowered my voice. "I was looking at puppy vids. But I'm glad you interrupted me. I have a lot of work to do."

She rolled her eyes. "You and your puppies. Hey, swing by at lunch, okay? I'm dying for a falafel." And she sauntered off, her hips testing the seams of her slim pencil skirt, and turning the heads of everyone in her wake.

I lowered my voice as soon as my BFF picked up. "Bridget!"

My boss wasn't big on personal phone calls, which sucked, because I made a lot of them.

"Crick! Whattup, girl?"

Hearing her greeting soothed me even though a massive amount of background noise was nearly drowning out her voice.

"Hi. Are you at the hospital?"

"Oh, god no. I just worked two twelve-hour shifts. I got the kids with me, and we're doing Brendan's least favorite thing in the world."

That made me snort-laugh. "Shopping?" I asked.

"You know it. Poor guy. I know he hates it, but he's growing so fast I gotta get him some new jeans. His others are halfway up his calves. The twins are in their stroller fighting over a toy. Ah, parenthood. So, how's D.C.?"

How *was* D.C.? That was a good question. Most days, I loved it. Today, not so much. And hearing Bridget's voice made me want to hop on the first flight back to Rhode Island, our home state where she still lived.

There was a time when I'd hoped she and her little guy Brendan would move down to D.C. with me. After her husband had passed away, it seemed like a new start was in order. But she stuck it out at home, facing her grief with a ballsiness I'd didn't think I'd ever have. That's when she met the second love of her life, Simon. A hot doctor with an even hotter British accent.

And they made the cutest fucking babies.

Talk about happy endings. Or would that be beginnings?

But I couldn't go back to Rhode Island, no matter

how shitty my day had been. That would be admitting failure. And I had too damn much pride for that.

I could see it now.

Cricket Curtain, local go-getter who'd financed a very expensive education at George Washington University, and who'd finagled her way into a sweet internship at the internationally renowned Washington Chronicle that eventually turned into a real job, has returned home to Rhode Island.

Yeah, no.

Not that there was anything wrong with our smallest state. I loved it. Visiting, that was. But I'd leveraged so much to get to D.C. where I'd hoped to become a star journalist. Going back was unthinkable.

And there were certain people who would get a lot of satisfaction from that. Especially my mother.

Seemed like there was always someone waiting to kick you when you're down.

Thus, my stubborn streak.

And then, there were the puppies. Volunteering at DogHouse was the highlight of my week. Walking the little fur babies, playing with them—even scooping up their poop—I loved it all.

"... and Simon has been on call at the hospital all week, so we've not seen each other, and let me tell you, I am *seriously* missing him if you know what I mean..."

I hadn't been listening to a word she was saying.

"You know, Brendan's school trip is to D.C. this fall. How 'bout if I come as a chaperone and stay a few days after?"

"On my god, yes! That would be so awesome. Do you think Simon will come, too?"

I had a not-so-secret crush on Simon. Everybody did. He was so funny and charming. And then there was his accent...

"Not sure yet if he'll be part of the trip. But if he isn't, we'll still have a great time. Hey, and don't forget that Block Island's coming up. It will be so awesome, and Simon's never been there."

"Yeah..." I said wistfully.

"*Go into the dressing room and try these on right now. I mean it, Brendan,*" she said in a stern mom-voice. Then she turned her attention back to me. "So, why're you so down in the dumps? I can hear it in your voice."

I peered over the wall of my cube to make sure no one was around, especially Wayne.

"Oh, you know. Still stuck doing obits. It's been three years now."

"C'mon, something will open up at some point," she said, like she had a hundred times before.

Just like I told myself every morning when I woke up.

"I know, I know. It's just that, sometimes it's hard to stay hopeful." I lowered my voice to a whisper. "And my boss is a weirdo. Did you know he goes to funerals for fun?"

"What? Nobody does that!"

"*Mom, these are stupid,*" Brendan moaned in the background.

She sighed. "*Yeah, sweetie, they are stupid. Let's pay for them and get out of here. We can go get frozen yogurt.*"

"I'd better let you go," I said.

"All right, honey, hang in there. I know something will open up for you, and you'll bust open the next Watergate scandal."

We'd been best friends since elementary school and had been there for each other through every disaster life had visited on us, including the car accident that had changed our lives. I was a lucky bitch to have her and her unwavering support.

I just needed to believe in myself the same way she did.

Although I'd planned to volunteer at DogHouse that night, I'd overheard some of my coworkers talk about going out for drinks.

I didn't particularly feel like drinks because I was really looking forward to the pups who didn't care what I did for a living, and whether or not I was living up to my potential. But if I wanted to get ahead at the paper, I needed to create strong, respectful, and lasting relationships with the people I worked with.

At least, that's what I'd read in my favorite career Facebook group, *Getting Ahead Without Giving Head*.

And, as an added bonus to the evening's activities, there was the promise of the paper's *editor in chief* popping in for a beer. I might be able to exchange a few words with him and make a good impression. Best of all, he always picked up the tab.

Free beer and career advancement. Just what the doctor ordered.

I heard the group assembling by the elevators, and while I hadn't been expressly invited, I sure as hell acted like I had been.

I threw on my cross-body bag, locked down my computer, and ran to catch up.

"Hey, guys," I said breathlessly, as if I'd been working on something super important up 'til the last minute and they were very lucky I'd finished in time so I could join.

"Oh, hey, Cricket. Didn't know you were coming." The perky little blonde looking me up and down was Sadie Magill, whom I secretly called Cruella de Vil.

"Wouldn't miss it, Sadie," I said with all the confidence I had.

I tagged after the group as we headed to Murphy's, the nearest Irish pub featuring cheap happy hour beers. I inserted myself into any conversation I could.

"Hey, Ed, how do you think the new trade agreement will impact interest rates?"

The paper's political reporter turned to me in surprise.

Folks in the obits department weren't usually interested in economics.

"Well, Cricket, it remains to be seen..."

I pretty much blocked out his answer after the first five seconds. I had no freaking idea what he was talking about.

Maybe I was trying *too* hard.

After we'd sat down at a splintery picnic table full of carvings of obscenities and other sentiments, Sadie leaned toward me. "So, Cricket, how are things in the obits department? I understand people are just dying to get into your column."

The entire table erupted in laughter at a joke I must have heard a thousand times before. Seriously, some new jokes about obituaries were desperately needed.

I leaned forward, so I could address her directly. "Don't worry, Sadie, we're saving a spot especially for you when your time comes."

The smile faded from her face as the table erupted in laughter again.

Chalk one up for *me*.

Our business reporter, Harry, turned to Ed. "Hey, have you you heard about that new guy elected to the Senate? Talbot Richardson's his name. Youngest senator ever elected. He turned thirty *during* the campaign."

"Shit, he just made it in under the wire," Ed said.

I had little interest in politics, a fact I successfully hid, so I hadn't paid much attention to the latest election. But the name Talbot Richardson did sound familiar.

Very familiar.

"Um, Ed, do you know where the new senator went to college?" I asked.

"Yeah, I was just reading his bio. Not much on it because he's so young, but he went to George Washington University, right here in D.C."

Oh. My. God.

Talbot Richardson.

The unrequited crush of my college years.

Holy shit. *He* was just elected to the U.S. Senate?

I worked for the Washington Chronicle and didn't fucking know that?

Talbot Richardson?

He was only the most handsome, charismatic guy on campus.

"It's the coolest thing, that he got elected" I said breezily, like I was completely in-the-know. "I know him from college."

I waved over the waitress for another beer, like I announced every day I'd gone to college with important and famous people.

And, as I'd hoped, all the heads turned in my direction.

"Nice guy," I said. "Very nice guy. I couldn't be happier for him."

Sadie leaned over the table again, the ends of her blonde hair dipping in a puddle of beer. "You know him from college? Are you *serious*?"

I nodded, not interested in deconstructing what it really meant to *know* someone. To discourage further questions, I took a gulp of my beer and looked at my watch.

Oh, fuck it.

I doubled down.

"He was so awesome. I mean, I had a couple classes with him, and we always sat in the back of the room and made fun of the teachers."

I had the attention of everyone at the table.

I ran with it. "I pretty much helped him get through calc, and he helped me with Spanish. He was in *love* with my roommate."

Okay, I needed to shut up. I was getting carried away.

"That's so cool," Harry said. "Tell us what he was like."

Uh oh. I couldn't resist.

"Um, well, he was really funny and down to earth. Liked sports. And of course, we all know how good-looking he is today. Well, you should have seen him back then."

I looked at the women around the table, who nodded in agreement.

"I mean, amiright, ladies?" I threw my head back and laughed like I was having the time of my life.

I sort of was, actually.

On a normal day, my coworkers paid little to no attention to me. How would I ever get ahead if I wasn't even on their radar? And at that moment in time, they were hanging on my every word.

Time to strike while the iron was hot.

I turned to Ed, the political reporter. "Hey, we were going to prepare an obit for each of the Supreme Court justices. Would you be able to help me with that?"

Perfect.

Of course, he'd want to collaborate with me. What an opportunity.

But, he wrinkled his nose. "Oh, god no. I don't want to work on those creepy before-they're-dead obits. That's so morbid."

He turned back to Harry and continued their discussion about interest rates.

Strike that.

The group began to disband, starting with Sadie, who had to get home to feed her kids and do homework. I split while I was still feeling like a big shot, claiming to have an early morning.

An early morning in obits? Um, right.

I cheerfully told everyone I'd see them in the morning and ran for the Metro with the kind of smile on my face that I hadn't had in *way* too long.

CHAPTER TWO

TALBOT

"It's not looking good, Talbot. I'm sorry I don't have better news."

Fuck.

Fuck. Fuck. Fuck.

I looked at my attorney, the same one my family had used for years, and the same one I'd known all my life. He was looking his age now, at seventy-two, but his bespoke suits and expensive haircuts kept him surrounded by young babes.

Well, it didn't hurt that he was rich as fuck, either.

"Damn, Damian." I leaned forward in my seat and dropped my head into my hands. There wasn't anything else to say. I shook my head as a migraine circled my temples like a hungry vulture.

"I know, Tal. Being a public figure is no walk in the

park. You gotta be careful at every turn. But I'm sure you know that from your father."

Not exactly. I mean, no psycho had come out of the woodwork and appointed my father her baby daddy the moment he was elected to the Senate. No, my father had not gone through anything like I was, at that moment.

Damian took a deep breath. "Here's my question for you, Tal. I hate to ask this, but as your attorney, I have to. Is there any way you *could* be the father of this woman's child?"

My head snapped up out of my hands, and I narrowed my eyes. Damian might have been my family attorney for as long as I could remember, but that didn't guarantee him a free pass to say whatever the hell he wanted.

And he saw that in my face, real quick.

His hands flew up like a *stop* sign. "Tal, relax. I'm just doing my job. C'mon. We all know you haven't exactly been living the life of a monk, if you know what I mean."

Fine. He had a point. I fucked around. A lot.

In my past.

"I know what you're getting at, Damian, and you're right. I've known a lot of women. But I remember them. This one, I've definitely never met."

He nodded, relieved his earlier question didn't escalate into the ugliness it could have.

Yeah, I'd let him off the hook. He was lucky I had.

My migraine had made its landing. Fuck all. And I had a big day ahead. "It's a set-up, Damian. I know it is."

"It's looking like that, Tal. Here's what we're gonna do. I have a great private investigator on retainer. He's the best of the best. I'll get him going on this. In addition, the DNA test results take three to five days, but so far, she's been stalling. That's a big red flag."

I'd been sworn in to the United States Senate only the day before. By five o'clock, the psycho had planted her story all over social media.

Yup. Within hours of swearing my allegiance to the country, someone was already trying to fuck with me.

I knew who was behind it. I mean, I didn't have any proof yet, but with Damian's help, I'd get to the bottom of it.

Plain and simple, it was my opponent. The prick who'd run a dirty fucking campaign against me. He was mad.

Mad that I won, despite his sleazeball tactics. But he had no one to blame except himself. Voters don't take kindly to sleaze, and this guy had brought it on in abundance.

Give a jerk enough rope, and he'll hang himself, had never been truer.

"You know it's Carlotti, right?" I asked.

Damian sat back in his chair, tapping the pads of his fingertips together, carefully choosing his words.

"Now, Talbot, be careful about accusing people.

That can get you into more trouble than this whole baby thing."

I wasn't so sure about that. Even though the DNA test would eventually prove I was telling the truth, there would still be a lasting mark against my name due to the sensitivity of the accusation—a mark that wouldn't disappear for a long, long time. I could do most anything and people would forget about it the next day. But the baby daddy accusation would stick. That's why my opponent had chosen it.

"There's one more thing, Talbot. I don't want you speaking to the press until we have more answers."

Shit, I had calls with several reporters already scheduled for the day. *The New York Times, Chicago Tribune...*

I texted my chief of staff while Damian was still talking.

bruce, cancel all media calls. fill you in soon as I'm back in the office

I actually should have texted the press secretary Bruce had just hired for me, but I didn't know the bastard's name yet. I hadn't even met him, now that I thought about it.

I stood to head out of the office, but Damian stopped me.

He extended his hand. "Talbot. I know I probably don't need to say this, but keep it in your pants. You're a national figure now, and there's peril around every corner."

I had to try not to laugh at that one. I mean, it was probably true, but to put it that way...

"Thanks. Looks like I'll be leaving it in my pants for a long time."

Yeah, right.

I hurried out of Damian's K Street office, where all the behind-the-scenes movers and shakers hung their hats —lawyers, lobbyists, ex-Congressmen, and the like— and caught a cab.

"Hart Senate Building, please."

The cabbie kept looking at me in the rearview mirror, probably trying to figure out if I was on somebody's staff or an actual elected member of Congress.

It had only been the previous evening that my mother had called me, having been the first in the family to hear about the baby daddy bullshit. *I* hadn't even heard it yet.

"Talbot, honey," she said the moment I picked up my cell phone.

"Hey. Mom. What's up?"

A sob exploded from the other end of the line.

"HOW COULD YOU?" she screamed.

Jesus.

"Mom, what's wrong. Is Dad there?"

Another sob, followed by a string of garbled words.

"Mom, I can't understand you. What the hell is going on?" Had someone died?

"You know, Talbot," she gasped through her tears, "your father and I have given you opportunity after opportunity. You've had the best of everything. A life of privilege. And *this* is how you thank us?"

For Christ's sake, I'd just been sworn into the U.S. Senate that morning. If that didn't make her happy, what the fuck would?

"Mom, I'm not following. Take a deep breath and tell me what happened."

"Why don't *you* tell me what happened?" she shrilled.

Being reasonable was getting me nowhere. Time to harness the big guns. I'd grown up with the woman, and I knew her theatrics like a repeat TV show.

"Mom, if you're not going to tell me what's going on, I'm going to end this call. You are so upset you aren't even making sense. Where's Dad, anyway?"

He could usually get her under control.

Dad was suddenly on the line. "Son, I want to give you the benefit of the doubt, but this is not looking good."

"*What. Is. Not. Looking. Good?* If you don't tell me, I'm going to hang up."

"So, you haven't heard?"

"Heard WHAT?"

"You've been accused of fathering a child out of

wedlock. It just came out in the press within the last hour."

The taste of expensive red wine soured in my mouth.

Fathering? A child? Out of wedlock? The jumble of words that had just come out of my dad's mouth weren't making any sense.

So I thought them through again.

Holy shit.

Was I somebody's goddamn baby daddy?

I looked up from the memo one of my staff had drafted for me. I still wasn't sure who was who in the office, even though they were all my employees. I'd let Bruce, my chief of staff, do my hiring because I just didn't have the patience for it. As a result, I didn't know who anybody was, or what they were supposed to do for me.

"Dude, we got Redskins tickets!" he said, barging into my office.

Now that he'd staffed up my team, he was clearly ready to enjoy some of the perks of working for me.

I, on the other hand, was not sure this guy knew how to stay out of trouble.

Easy thing for me to say, the alleged baby daddy.

I took a deep breath. "Bruce, you cannot accept every damn thing someone offers us. There are these things called ethics rules. Learn them before you ruin both our careers."

His face fell. Sometimes, I wondered why I'd brought him on board to be my second in command, aside from the fact that he was my closest friend and confidant. He'd almost singlehandedly gotten me elected in spite of all the shit Carlotti had thrown my way, but Christ, I needed to rein him in like he was a toddler.

He plopped down in the seat opposite me and looked around, holding a notebook in his hand as if he might take notes.

Bruce never took notes.

"God, this office is butt ugly."

I followed his gaze. He was right. I mean, I'm sure it was somebody's taste but certainly not mine. It looked like something out of George Washington's house with the old, heavy furniture, stuffy sofas and chairs, and heavy blue curtain swags dripping with gold trim.

Guess they'd never heard of contemporary design.

"So, Tal, you'll never guess who I just saw," he said, changing the subject.

Without waiting for me to guess, he jumped into his story.

"You know that senator from last year who got into all that trouble? He was dating some woman who took a bunch of sex pics of the two of them, and then she posted them on social media? That's who I just saw. I think it was Senator Winestock. Yeah, I think that was his name."

I couldn't say anything about someone else's transgressions—I was embroiled in my own, which were about to explode into a shitshow of epic proportions.

He continued. "In case you haven't noticed, this place is loaded with hot babes. Seriously. Have you seen the press secretary I hired for you? I don't know how I'm gonna keep my dick in my pants."

Of course he'd hired a hot woman. That was just like him.

He leaned back into his chair like he'd won the lottery. "Fuck me. This D.C. shit is gonna rock."

"Bruce, you remember I grew up around this stuff—and that my dad was a senator, right? So, I just want to remind you to keep your shit together. Do not fuck any of our staff or so help me, you'll be out of a job so goddamn fast you won't know what hit you."

The corner of his mouth turned up as he considered what I was saying.

I nodded for emphasis. "Yeah. It's that serious. I'm already in a world of hurt because of this baby daddy bull. Even though we'll prove the woman is lying, this shit will follow me around for a long time. And who's to say Carlotti doesn't have something else up his sleeve? The fucker's going to do his damnedest to ruin me, that's how bitter he is. We have to be completely irreproachable. Not a single wrong move or we're screwed. Do you understand that?"

He nodded slowly. "You're right. That fucker's gonna be poised to take us down at almost any price. Is Damian sending out a P.I. to dig around?"

"Yeah. Of course. But I can't do any interviews until he gives me the go ahead. No press."

He grimaced and shook his head. "You know Anderson Cooper wants to talk to you. I don't know what format he has in mind, but c'mon, you at least have to meet with him. He's the shit."

"I can't, Bruce. Tell him, and everyone else, I'm not allowed to talk to the press on the advice of my attorney. They'll understand. It's not forever. Just until we sort this all out."

Christ, was this my new life? Assholes waiting to take me down every chance they got?

"Gotcha," Bruce said. "I'll take care of it."

He stood to go. "I need to set up our first staff meeting. But hey, we were also invited to go sailing on the Potomac."

Had he not heard a damn thing I'd just said?

"We'll have time to have fun, Bruce, don't you worry. But we have to start off slow given the bullshit I'm dealing with right now."

He stopped at the carved double doors that led to the outer office. This place would be a traditionalist decorator's wet dream.

"Hey, I got a question for ya," he said. "What makes you so sure you're *not* the baby daddy? I mean, we'll know in a few days, theoretically, but you know, you have been quite the man whore. And I mean that in the best possible way." If he wasn't grinning so broadly, I might have had to hit him.

"Damian asked me the same thing. You all act like I'm a dog in heat. I may mess around with a lot of women, but I remember them. And this woman, I never met. Carlotti should have found someone I actually *knew*."

"Yeah, he should have. But that doesn't mean he won't try to in the future. All the more reason to keep our noses clean. Problem is, we've never been too good at that, have we?" he asked.

"Time to learn, brother."

CHAPTER THREE

CRICKET

I was doing my best to look cool, like I had meetings with the editor in chief of the Chronicle every day. I smiled at Ken, hoping I didn't look like a grinning idiot, and tugged at the hem of my skirt, which exposed the fuzzy knees I hadn't shaved in ages.

"So, Cricket, how long have you been with the paper now?" he asked, the little crinkles around his eyes relaxing me.

He really was a good guy. Underneath his pretentiousness, that was.

"Oh gosh, let me see. I've been in obits three years now, and before that was my six-month internship. Also in obits."

Why was he asking this? Was I getting fired?

Or maybe promoted?

Maybe he'd seen my dedication to the paper, my excellent research skills, and my ability to spin a yarn out of something not actually very interesting. Perhaps all this was finally going to pay off.

Or, maybe he was displeased with my progress on writing obits for the Supreme Court justices. I mean, I knew they were time-sensitive—some of those folks were old as dirt and could kick the bucket any day. We really needed to be ready. But I could move that stuff to the top of my priority pile. All he had to do was say the word.

I was a team player. Seriously.

He walked toward me and propped his ass on the corner of his massive, cluttered desk.

This was not good. Not at all.

I couldn't afford to get fired. No, I had mountains of student loan debt hanging over my head. Shit, I'd have to move in with my mother, back in Rhode Island.

Wouldn't she just get a ton of satisfaction out of that?

And, once I was fired from the Washington Chronicle, no other paper would ever want me. I was sure of it.

"How are things going for you? Here at the paper?" he asked.

I smiled brilliantly. "Great. Really great. Wayne's an awesome boss, even if he does like going to funerals for fun. We're just getting the work done. You know?"

He tilted his head at me. "You finding it interesting? You want to stay in obits forever, like Wayne?"

I gulped. This was the chance I'd been waiting for. Don't mess it up.

I took a deep breath. "It has been a great avenue for working my way into journalism. I've learned so much, and I think I've done pretty good work. But I would like to move into the newsroom at some point. Politics, business, any of those areas."

Okay, I pulled that last bit out of my ass. I didn't know a goddamn thing about either politics or business.

But I'd learn. Fast.

He nodded. "Good to know. Good to know. Hey, sorry I missed happy hour last night. Got hung up on a call with the Vice President," he said.

Of *course* he did.

He crossed his arms, like everyone in the news business did. Made them look serious but approachable. "So, word has it you know our new senator from New York, Talbot Richardson."

Oh. *That's* what this is about?

This, I could handle.

"Talbot, yup. Went to GW with him. Nice guy." I nodded, trying not to repeat my verbal diarrhea of the night before.

Ken scratched his beard, like he always did before asking a question. "How well did you know him?"

"Oh, well... I knew him. I mean, I *know* him. Ya know."

Shit. Where was this going?

He clapped his hands together and walked back to his chair.

"Perfect," he said, leaning on his desk with his elbows. "Since you know him, you're probably aware of the paternity suit that came out a couple days ago."

What? Really? I didn't know a thing about that. Holy shit. You'd think I'd read the goddamn paper I worked for.

"Oh, yeah," I said, lying my ass off. "What a mess."

He glanced at his watch. Was this all he wanted, to ask me about Talbot Richardson? I thought the editor in chief of the Washington Chronicle was a busy man.

Turned out that no, that was not all he wanted.

Ken began shifting the piles on his desk. "So, since he's been embroiled in this mess, he isn't granting interviews, at least, not for the time being. And we were really hoping to talk to him. You know, he's the youngest person ever elected to the U.S Senate. It would make a good story for the paper."

I nodded with enthusiasm. "I know. How cool, right?" I gushed.

"Cricket, I'd like you to reach out to him and set up an interview. You know, since you went to school with him and are friends."

Oh. Shit.

"You mean, *I* would interview him? *I* would write up the story?" My heart was beginning to race, and I bounced back and forth between elation and pure terror.

He shrugged. "Sure. Why not? You're ready for something new, and since you guys are buddies, it seems like a no-brainer. I'm sure he'll accommodate an old college pal."

He stood and opened his office door, a signal that our meeting was over.

"Gotta go, Cricket. I'm having lunch with the Secretary of Labor in five minutes. He's godfather to my youngest."

He looked down, shaking his head, like he couldn't believe his luck.

Yeah, I couldn't believe *my* fucking luck, either.

The chance I'd been waiting for. All based on my own bullshit lies.

Back at my desk, I went to my favorite puppy website. I scrolled through all the labs and then moved to the hybrids like Labradoodles until I felt a little calmer.

In reality, though, what I should have been looking at were job search sites because I was quite sure I'd be out on the street very soon.

Talbot Richardson was not going to grant me any kind of interview, not in this lifetime, or in the next. Why?

Because he didn't know me from a hole in the wall.

Out 'friendship' consisted of my following him around campus to see which dorm he lived in and which class he had at eight a.m. on Wednesdays.

Oh, and I might have stalked him in the dining hall, too. Turned out he ate a lot of grilled cheese.

That was the extent of our 'relationship.'

And now, thanks to my big mouth, the Washington Chronicle was counting on me to do a story on him because he wasn't granting anyone else interviews.

Ken's assumption that Talbot would meet with me was perfectly logical. I mean, if he and I had really gone college together, how could he possibly turn me down?

Problem was, in all my years of crushing on him at GW, I don't think he looked my way once. Not once.

But this was my big chance, and it might be the only one I got.

Next time, I'd keep my big goddamn mouth shut when tempted to brag about people I didn't fucking know.

After the puppy pics, I Googled Talbot. He was even more handsome than he'd been in college, and of course, there were endless photos of him with stunning women on his arm.

I couldn't begin to imagine the life he led, where doors opened for him everywhere he went. Shit, the sea probably parted for him, too.

Rich, good-looking, family connections, dad a former senator. A mountain of privilege I could only begin to imagine.

One article I found on Google referred to him as your 'quintessential boy next door.'

Sure, if you lived next door to gods.

"Cricket."

As usual, I nearly jumped out of my skin.

It was Wayne, giving me another heart attack.

"Oh, hey, Wayne. I'm starting to crank on those new obits. I'm sure I'll have something to show you tomorrow," I lied.

He shifted uncomfortably. "That's not what I stopped by for."

"No?"

He took a deep breath. "I was wondering why Ken wanted to see you in his office."

Cripes, he knew I'd spoken with Ken? Were there no secrets in the damn place?

I decided to play it cool. "Oh, he was just asking me about Talbot Richardson, the new member of the Senate."

I was committed to ending my verbal diarrhea, which had already put my career on the road to ruin.

I turned back to my computer, hoping he'd take the hint and split. But no such luck.

"What *about* Talbot Richardson? Why was he asking you anything about him?"

I just knew he'd be bent out of shape that someone at the top had taken the time to speak to me. So, I decided to throw him a bone.

"We went to GW together. That's all. Nothing big." I left it at that.

"Uh huh," Wayne said, as if he'd figured out something important. "What about it?"

Persistent fucker.

"Ken, um, wants me to interview him and do a story on him."

I braced myself.

The color faded from Wayne's already-pale face. "He *what?* What's that all about? You're not the political reporter. And besides, you have enough to do here in obits. Ken has no right to take away my most important resource."

I wasn't thrilled at being thought of as a 'resource,' but the 'most important' part felt okay. Furthermore, Ken was the editor in chief. He could do whatever the hell he wanted to, and that included pulling rank on his underlings whenever he saw fit.

While Wayne continued to hover, I opened Google and began to pull down biographies of the Supreme Court Justices I had yet to write obits for. At the rate I was going, they'd all be dead and gone before I got any words on paper.

"Well," Wayne said. "Keep me posted."

"Oh, I will. I'll have something to you shortly," I said, throwing him a smile over my shoulder.

"No, I meant keep me posted on the senator."

"Sure, Wayne, no problem."

I dug into my file of old obits and picked out some nice paragraphs that could be recycled, the kind of words that offered a positive and joyous perspective on a life. This, with some personal details of the deceased, always made a great obit.

Last year, Wayne had permitted me to attend an annual conference for obituary writers. I picked up some good tips there in spite of some of the characters in attendance. I didn't know if they went to funerals for fun like Wayne, but a lot of them seemed pretty pleased to essentially be the town criers of death.

A moniker I could live without.

By the end of the day, I had pretty solid drafts of five new obits and planned to pull together the next five in the morning. With that under my belt, I needed to come up with some ways to get the new Senator Talbot Richardson to not only talk to me but also give me an on-the-record interview for the Washington Chronicle.

Of course, I knew the chances of that happening were lower than a snowball's chance of surviving in hell, but I had to give it a shot.

The question was, how do you get a shot at something that's so far out of the realm of possibility that it's in another galaxy?

I'd stalked Talbot Richardson before. I could do it again. 'Course, I was in college back then, and the stakes were much lower. I was a nobody, and he was just a good-looking student with a famous dad.

Now he was a senator, and I worked for one of the

country's most prestigious newspapers—even if I was currently in the obits department.

But I'd give it my best shot.

First, I had to find out where he lived. Then, maybe I could 'accidentally' deliver him a pizza or some such. I could just see it.

Oh, hi, I thought this was Rebecca's place. We're going to eat this delicious pizza tonight. Say, don't I know you from somewhere...

Or maybe I could be crossing the street and pretend he hit me with his car.

Oh, my god, you almost killed me. My back, my back! Hey, did you go to college at GW...

If I got really desperate, I could pretend to be his cleaning lady.

Hi, yeah, I clean houses on the side to help pay off the giant student loans I incurred while in college at GW. What, you went there, too? Ya know, I think I might remember you...

Okay. I wasn't desperate yet, but I was glad to know I had options should I end up in that situation. The ideas were crystallizing, and I knew with a little scouting I could get my sorry ass in front of the guy.

The question was, how would I get him to talk?

CHAPTER FOUR

TALBOT

More fucking ugly colonial architecture. I was surrounded by it.

I'd once read that the actor Billy Bob Thornton had a phobia about antiques. I knew no more than that aside from the fact that I'd always thought it was strange as hell.

I mean, who's afraid of an old piece of furniture?

Well, now I was beginning to understand the poor bastard's affliction. And if I didn't make some changes to my physical surroundings, I, too, would end up with a phobia of the very architecture and design D.C. was built on. Just what everyone around me seemed to love.

Was something wrong with *me* or with *them*?

Unfortunately, the Georgetown row house I'd rented

was just as hideous as my Senate office. Sorely missing, in both places, were the high ceilings and wide-open living space of my industrial-chic loft home in lower Manhattan.

My new living arrangements hemmed me in, like the walls were creeping toward me, waiting to encase me like Edgar Allen Poe's *Tell-Tale Heart*.

I needed to get a grip. But with all the bullshit around my baby daddy drama, I couldn't help but look over my shoulder all day long. I knew Carlotti and how he operated, and I knew if he didn't manage to take me down with this scandal, he'd have ten more up his sleeve just waiting.

Miserable son of a bitch.

But I'd think about that bastard later. He'd get what he had coming to him, one way or the other.

In the meantime, I needed to prepare for a meeting the next morning, scheduled for the ungodly hour of seven a.m., with the entire Senate.

I'd already met a few of the folks I'd be serving alongside, and I knew a couple pretty well through my father. But I was really hoping to find some strong allies who had the same vision I did and who were committed to making some real change.

Actually, a lot of things around me needed to fucking change.

∾

"Damian, give me some good news," I said into my speakerphone

I propped my feet up on top of my massive desk. Papers shuffled in the background of my lawyer's office.

"I've got my P.I. on the case, Talbot, and hope for some substantial information in the next few days. We'll find out what's behind the... um... accusation."

Something about his hesitation hit me the wrong way.

I moved my feet off my desk and began to pace the office, barely registering the view of the Capitol Building in the distance.

Finally, it struck me. Damian didn't believe me. He thought I *was* the baby daddy. Or at least, he had some doubt.

Did everyone else doubt my denials of the charge, too? Like my parents and friends?

And my voters?

Fuck.

I could only imagine what the other senators would be thinking during our meeting this morning. Looking me right in the eye and thinking I *was* a dirty dog. I could just see it now.

I leaned over the phone to hang up the call. "Damian, I gotta run. You got anything else for me?"

"Nope. Just... keep up the good work."

Fucker. I knew what he wanted to say.

Keep it in your pants, Talbot...

Guess that's the price of being a man-whore.

Just as I was heading out, there was a barely-perceptible knock on my office door.

A head peeked through. My new press secretary. At least, that's who I thought it was.

"Senator Richardson?"

I pulled the door open the rest of the way and waved her in. "Good morning."

"Um, morning, Senator."

Shit. What was her name again?

I grabbed my suit jacket and straightened my tie. "I'm heading out to a meeting. What can I do for you?"

"Well, Anderson Cooper's office is still trying to get you to agree to an interview," she said.

Just then, Bruce burst in.

"Dude, you gotta talk to Anderson—"

He saw the press secretary behind the door.

"Oh, good morning, Rose."

Rose. Her name was Rose.

I nodded toward her. "Rose was just telling me Cooper's office has been in touch. But I'm still on a press embargo. Can't meet with anyone, according to my attorney."

She stepped forward and placed something on my desk, then backed up. Fuck, did she think I was going to get her pregnant, too?

"Sir, to that end, I've put together a statement explaining the... um, whole situation, that we can use with the press until further notice."

I grabbed her memo and tucked it into my suit

pocket.

"Thanks, Rose. I'll read it on my way to my meeting."

She scurried out the door like she might catch an STD.

"Bruce, why is that girl so afraid of me?" I asked.

He shrugged. "I gotta tell you, Tal, the rumor mill is flying. I'm concerned other women are going to come out of the woodwork and point their fingers at you. When all is said and done, you might have ten fucking kids."

He dropped his head back and laughed his ass off.

I was dying to knock that joke right off his face.

"Yeah, yeah. Fuck you, Bruce. We have to get this under control. No wonder the press secretary ran off. She's probably never dealt with anything like this. How old is she, anyway? Can you please stop hiring people who look like teenagers?"

Already late for my first meeting, I started walking through the office and realized that I didn't know half the people working for me.

Bruce jogged to keep up as we worked our way through the halls of the Senate Building.

"Tal, I know she's kind of green, but did you see the ass on her?" he whispered.

I nodded in greeting as I passed a group of school kids on a tour.

"Bruce, you need to calm down."

To think people were telling *me* to keep it in my

pants. Christ.

I stopped walking to make my point clear. "This is not spring break, Bruce. Clean up your language at work. And stop looking at the females in the office that way. It will not lead to anything good, I promise you."

I continued walking.

"Okay, but what do I do about Anderson Cooper?"

I stopped again, raking my hand through my hair.

Another habit I'd need to drop. My father had told me it wasn't *senatorial*. Whatever the hell that meant.

I remembered the statement Rose had asked me to review.

"Here, let's look at what Rose prepared." I unfolded the paper as we stepped into an elevator that was, fortunately, empty.

Office of U.S. Senator Talbot Richardson

Please note that during the investigation into the paternity claim against Senator Richardson, he will not be taking any meetings with the press on advice from counsel. When the DNA results are in, an announcement will be made.

Thank you for understanding.

"To the point. I like it," I said, handing the paper to Bruce. "Have Rose send it out. And tell Cooper to be patient. I'll meet with him as soon as I can."

I took off for my meeting, leaving Bruce to jog back to the office.

Later in the day, when I was plowing through a stack of briefing documents someone had piled on my desk, my office door creaked open.

"Senator Richardson? May I come in?"

An attractive young woman planted herself well into my office, not waiting for my answer.

I had no idea what she wanted or who she was, but I needed a break, anyway. "What can I do for you?" I asked.

She minced her way toward me, tottering on skyscraper heels, and planted herself in front of my desk. I'd quickly learned that if people helped themselves to a chair, they were much more likely to stay longer. So, I'd made a deal with my admin, Evelyn, to keep my chairs piled with papers and books, which she would remove if I had a meeting scheduled where I actually *wanted* people to take their time.

"Hi, Senator," she said softly.

Fuck, what was her name? And what did she do for me? Legislative aide? Network stuff?

Oh, to hell with it.

"I'm sorry, but can you tell me your name again?" I asked.

Her face fell, but only for a moment. "Leisl. Like the character in *The Sound of Music*."

Oh, hell no. I hated that corny movie.

"What can I do for you, Leisl?"

She worked her way around the side of my desk, and there was no doubt in my mind what was coming next.

Like I didn't already have enough problems. The modern-day Leisl was a dirty girl.

"Senator—or can I call you Talbot?"

I leaned back in my chair, waiting for the right moment to kick her out of my office.

"You may call me Senator."

"Oh. Okay. Well, Senator, I know you're new in town and probably don't know many people..."

She ran a red lacquered finger along a groove in my desk, then propped one of her ass cheeks up on the edge of it.

And then, she parted her thighs just enough to let me see she wasn't wearing any panties. Oh, and she was shaved down there, too.

For fuck's sake.

I got up and crossed to the door, which I yanked open. I caught the eye of Evelyn, who sat just outside my office, as she looked up in alarm. She jumped to her feet.

"Leisl, I'm sorry to tell you, but this is not happening. We will not be spending time together socially. Ever. But thank you for asking."

If Evelyn's eyebrows rose any higher, I think they would have flown over her forehead. Which was the reaction I was hoping for. I needed her to hear the whole thing.

Leisl turned beet red, apparently not used to being turned down.

"But Senator—"

I opened the door wider and gestured toward the outer hallway. "Thanks, Leisl. I'll see you later at the staff meeting."

A dark cloud crossed her face, and she stomped out in a blur.

Evelyn approached me, speaking quietly. "Everything okay, Senator?"

"Yeah. I guess so. Let's not let her in my office again when I'm alone, okay?"

She pressed her thin lips together, tight little lines surrounding them. "I knew that one was trouble, Senator. I'll take care of it." She patted me on the arm and pulled my door closed.

I fell back into my office chair, a little freaked at the close call. I mean, the girl was hotter than shit, there was no denying it. Of course she was. That was why Bruce had hired her. He probably didn't even know if she could fucking read.

But I already had a world of shit raining down on my head. My dad's corny saying, *don't dip your pen in the company inkwell*, echoed.

And one thing I did not need was another goddamn problem.

Then, Bruce came flying in. Of course.

"Hey, buddy, you're gonna have to learn how to knock," I said, frowning.

"Oh, fuck you, asshole. Hey, I just saw big tits running through the office crying. What happened?"

"I kicked her out, that's what happened. She sat right here on the corner of my desk and flashed me her pussy."

Bruce's mouth fell open. After his initial shock, he looked up at the ceiling and cackled.

When he finished laughing, he got excited. "Holy shit. I heard these D.C. babes were like that. All prim and proper on the outside with their power suits, pearls, and blonde bobbed hair, but when you get down to it, they are horny fucking bitches ready to suck any powerful cock they can get their mouths on."

Was he for real?

"Well, she won't be getting her mouth on mine. I want you to fire her first chance you get."

Bruce held his hands up like a *stop* sign. "Oh, hold on, partner. We can't just go and fire her because she wanted to get in your senatorial pants."

He burst out laughing again.

So I leaned over my desk to make my point.

"Look, asshole. This is the kind of attitude that got me into the trouble I'm in right now. She needs to go."

The smile slipped from his face. "We can't let her go. Her dad's one of your biggest donors."

Fuck. Fuck. Fuck. I should have known to expect something like this.

"Jesus. Going forward, do not hire anyone else we're beholden to. It leaves us in a shit position."

Just then, my phone buzzed, and Evelyn came over the intercom.

"Senator Richardson, it's your father," she said.

Bruce popped to his feet, grateful for the chance to escape my pissed off mood.

Before I answered my call, I pointed a finger at him. "The girl has got to go. I'm counting on you."

He gave me a thumbs up as he disappeared, which probably meant he either wasn't going to do a goddamn thing, or if he did, he was going to take his sweet time.

"Hi Dad," I said into my speakerphone.

"Talbot. How goes it?" he asked.

I sank into my chair. "Oh, it's been better."

My dad was not one to show compassion, but my tone must have wrung it out of him.

"I know, Son. I know."

Well, damn.

"Damian tells me the woman is procrastinating on doing the paternity test. That's a sign she's got something to hide. And he's also pretty sure she's not working alone," I said.

My father was silent for a moment. "You think it's Carlotti?" he asked.

"There's no doubt in my mind, Dad. Damian has a P.I. on both him and the woman. I just can't believe people go to these lengths for revenge. Miserable bastard."

"Son, he's the same way with me. For some reason,

he's had it in for those of us in the Richardson family for a long time."

"Yeah, well now the Richardson family has it in for *him*. Carlotti's gone too far this time."

Game on, motherfucker.

I laced up my expensive running shoes, pulled a baseball cap low on my forehead, and grabbed my sunglasses. Pounding the pavement was the best way I knew to blow off steam—better than booze, pep talks, and getting laid—and god knew my stress was piling up in spades. It had worked for me since my college days at George Washington University and hadn't failed me yet.

I headed for the old towpath along the Georgetown canal, planning to run until my lungs burned, my legs cramped, and I couldn't take another step. That's the only thing that would take my mind off the bullshit that was my life.

Pain. Sweet pain.

At least, that was my thought until I spotted a fellow runner on the trail with what appeared to be a twisted ankle. Short shorts and legs for miles. A firm tummy shown off by a sports bra holding what looked like a gorgeous pair of tits. Piles of red hair gathered into some messy sort of confection at her neck.

I desperately needed a hard run, but I couldn't leave a fellow jogger just sitting there, could I?

CHAPTER FIVE

CRICKET

In addition to being a debt-riddled obits writer for the Washington Chronicle, I could now add stalker to my resume.

And apparently, I was pretty damn good at it because Talbot Richardson was heading right my way.

New career, hello.

I'd sort of followed him home from work one day. Then, I'd sort of hung out across the street, pretending to be waiting for a ride, until he came back out. Then, I'd sort of followed him to the old towpath in Georgetown where he started to jog. My crazy idea was launched.

I'd meet him jogging. We'd talk and find out we'd been at college together. And then, I'd ask for the sale.

Interview time.

It had all been remarkably simple. Seriously. I did not understand why private investigators got paid so much money.

Actually, I did, once I thought about it.

They were awesome and pulled off shit like I was about to.

"Looks like you're having some trouble there," Talbot said, crouching with his hands on his knees.

With him so close, I could see he was even better looking than in college. And he'd been freaking beautiful then. Time had matured the angles of his face, defining it, and a few—a very few—gray hairs had sprung around his temples.

Christ, I might have tried to insert myself into this guy's life even if I *hadn't* been assigned to squeeze an interview out of him.

"Oh, hi. Yeah, I stepped on a rock. I guess I twisted my ankle." I pointed to my fake injury.

"Okay, let me help you to this wall over here." He put an arm around me, and I leaned into him, barely putting pressure on my 'bad' foot to continue my lame charade.

I'd made sure to fake a left foot sprain so I could still drive.

It seemed I was good at this deception shit.

When I was seated, he reached for my foot.

"We need to get this running shoe off before the swelling sets in."

Oh, shit. Swelling. How could I fake that?

"Good idea, thank you," I said.

He eased the shoe off my foot with more care than I deserved and then pulled my sock off.

His touch was so gentle it left my heart pounding, and even though I'd not jogged two steps, I had a little boob sweat going. I hadn't counted on him being so goddamned sexy.

He took my foot in his hand and turned it gently.

"Hmmm. No swelling yet. Maybe it won't be that bad of a sprain." He propped himself on the wall next to me.

"Yeah. Hopefully it won't be too bad. I hate to miss my runs." The lies were just piling up. "They keep me sane, you know what I mean?"

He pulled off his sunglasses and looked toward the Potomac, and I saw the blue eyes that had captivated me during my undergraduate days.

"I'm with ya on that."

I forced myself to look away before I became creepy staring girl. "Well, I don't want to keep you from your run. Thank you for helping me."

Please don't leave. Please don't leave.

"Well," he said, looking at his watch, "I've kind of run out of time now to do the big run I was thinking about. Besides, how are you going to get home? Where do you live?"

"In Southwest, but, I like to run here by the Potomac. My car is down by the river." I stood as if I were going to hop all the way down the hill.

It was the moment of truth.

"You can't possibly get there alone. Here, let me help you." He stood and put his arm around me to take the bulk of my weight. I wrapped an arm over his shoulders and realized I was touching nothing but hard muscle.

I was starting to feel badly about lying to this nice man. But only a little. I leaned into him and inhaled his scent, which was nothing more than clean guy and simple soap. Exactly how I liked it.

Wait, this wasn't about whether or not I liked this guy. I was on a mission.

I waved my free hand around as if I were a tour guide. "I love this part of Georgetown, don't you? It used to be all industrial here back in the day, but look at all these fancy condos now..."

I continued assaulting him with my verbal diarrhea as I clumsily step-hopped back to my car. Faking a sprained ankle was actually exhausting, and by the time we reached my car, I was dripping with sweat and not sure whether I'd remembered my deodorant that morning.

"You seem to know D.C. pretty well," he said as I pointed out my car.

Shit. Time was running out.

"Oh, I do. I went to college here. GW," I said.

He tilted his head and smiled. "Hey, I went to GW, too."

Okay. Now he was looking at me. Hard.

But he couldn't possibly remember me. I don't think he'd even looked at me the whole time we were in school.

"Ya know," I said, shaking my finger at him, "when you took off your sunglasses, I thought you looked familiar. Well, what a small world. Did you stay here after graduation?"

Like I didn't know exactly what he'd been doing...

"Um, I left for a while and recently moved back."

No kidding.

"Well, welcome back. D.C. is such a great place. Tell me what dorm you lived in," I demanded.

"Dakota."

Of course, I knew that, as well...

"Wow. I was in Lafayette. Right next to each other. I bet we ate in the dining room at the same time. Maybe that's where I saw you." I laughed and looked out over the Potomac, trying to look wistful for old college days.

The ones I was still paying for and would be for years to come.

I had to think quick. If I lost him now, I wasn't sure how I'd get in front of him again.

Christ, what I'd gone through just to get to this point. I'd started by calling his office and his extremely green press secretary blew me off, like I knew she would. Then, I followed him, from a great distance—

I'm not an idiot—as he went to a vote in the Capitol and then to a meeting, hoping that somehow, some way, we might be able to bump into each other and start talking.

But that was not to be. I don't know what I'd been thinking, but the guy was freaking busy. He didn't have time to chat with anyone, much less me. So, the next day, I waited in my car for him to pull out of the Senate parking garage and followed him across the city to Georgetown to scope out where he lived. I *actually* did that. I was officially desperate and pathetic.

Determining where he lived was half the battle. After I'd established that, it was relatively easy to figure out his running schedule. That brought me to my faked injury. If he hadn't stopped, but instead had just ignored me and started his run, I'd be back at the drawing board.

I felt shitty for being so deceitful.

Keep your eye on the ball, girl.

His kindness toward my fake sprained ankle took me by surprise. Even though I'd had a massive crush on him from afar in college, I'd always assumed he was a snobby douche-y sort of guy, which I'm embarrassed to admit made me like him more—hey, I never said I had good taste in men. So, his effort to get me to my car actually blew me away. I kind of wished he *hadn't* been so nice.

Nice, good-looking, *and* a U.S. senator. The perfect storm. The dude must have women lining up at his door. Seriously. He was the catch of the century. Maybe even millennia.

But that was okay. I wanted one thing from him, and it was something he could easily give. After that, all the other ladies could have him.

To stall for more time, I continued my onslaught of verbal diarrhea, babbling about the good old college days.

"What did you say your name was?" I asked innocently.

"Talbot," he said.

"Great." I extended my hand. "I'm Cricket. Cricket Curtain."

"Nice to meet you. Will you be okay from here?" he asked.

Shit. Should I ask? Should I go for it?

"I'm great. Thank you so much for your help."

It didn't feel right. Too contrived. I'd have to try again, some other way.

He glanced at his watch. "Looks like I have time for a quick run. I'm gonna take off. You take care, okay?"

Shit.

"Um, yeah. I'll be fine. Thank you, Talbot."

And he was gone, along with my hopes of getting the goddamn interview that was going to make my career.

CHAPTER SIX

Talbot

"Yo. Over here," I called across the basketball court to one of my buddies.

"Here ya go, asshole."

I stepped back, catching the ball Bruce threw just before it crashed into my sternum.

Douche.

I made a basket just to fuck with him, when another college buddy joined us on the court.

"Tal, how's it being a daddy before your time?" one of them said with a loud guffaw.

The other, Lou, dribbled the ball up away from me to the other end of the court.

"Fuck off." I told them.

They'd clearly underestimated the peril of annoying the shit out of me. Yeah, they were college buddies, but that didn't mean I'd be cutting them any slack on the court. We were all pretty evenly matched, but because they pissed me off, I was going to run them into the ground.

After I'd scored every point in our game, we collapsed into the bleachers at the community center where I coached kids' basketball. I wasn't sure yet that my work in the Senate would really allow me the time to continue with my volunteering, but I was damn sure going to try to make it work.

Truth be told, I never really wanted to be in the U.S. Senate. But it was my legacy—at least, that's what everyone else around me said.

If I'd had my way, sure I would have run for the Senate eventually, but my real dream had been to spend a few years in the Peace Corps on some sort of development project before doing anything else. But somehow, that dream got swept under the rug as I was moved into campaign mode by the same machine that had gotten my father elected back in the day. Next thing I knew, I'd won, having beaten the vengeful Carlotti.

Don't get me wrong, I was honored to have been elected, and especially to have beaten my scumbag opponent. His dad had run against mine many years ago, and the elder Carlotti never got over having lost. He remained pissed to this day, and it showed in his son's campaign against me.

The apple doesn't fall far from the tree and all that.

"So, how're you doing, really?" my buddy asked, catching his breath.

"Better than you, dude. Your face is beet red, and you can barely breathe. I guess having a wife and kids is not so great for your health. You're a walking advertisement for a heart attack in your thirties," I said.

He looked at his feet while he shook his head. "You got that right. I've never been so out of shape in my life. I've got no time. It's all diapers and play dates. I can't remember the last time I saw my wife naked."

At the moment, that sounded idyllic.

"Well, I'm living my goddamn life under a microscope. Every move I make is watched and dissected, and makes it to the evening news by seven P.M. Then there's the thrill of attracting psychos who pretend to be having my love child." I spun the basketball between my fingers until it balanced on one.

Bruce jumped in with his usual shit-eating grin. Was I going to regret having brought him in as my chief of staff?

"Yeah, well, it's not all bad. You should see some of the hotties up on Capitol Hill. Unreal."

"Really? Can I come by your office next week?"

"You guys all need to stop thinking with your little heads," I said.

"He's right, Bruce," Lou said. "Keep your nose clean or you'll be in a world of hurt. Washington, D.C. is not forgiving."

"Hey, Tal," Lou continued, "there's always YouPorn

and your hand. Maybe that will get you through your six-year term in the U.S. Senate."

That sent a wave of laughter through the guys.

Fuck that.

He slapped me on the back. "Dude, what's up with the DNA test? Won't that put everything to a rest?"

"Absolutely. But she's stalling. Which I think makes it pretty clear she has something to hide and that whoever put her up to this didn't think the whole shit-show through. Fucking idiots. Problem is, even when I'm exonerated, this will live on in my voters' minds. That's what really sucks."

The Peace Corps was looking more attractive by the moment. Who knew being elected would feel like imprisonment?

~

"Talbot. How are you?" a female voice called from behind me.

Well, look at that, right there in my neighborhood grocery.

"Cricket Curtain, right?"

I barely recognized the woman I'd helped on the towpath. I'd thought she looked good then, but now that she was in her civvies, she was downright hot as fuck in her skinny jeans and Washington Nationals baseball cap.

I was a sucker for the girl-next-door look—I

suppose because most of the women I met were social-climbing glamazons.

And damn if her tits weren't perfect in her stretchy, white tank top.

"I thought you lived over in Southwest. What are you doing in Georgetown?"

She blushed a little. Fucking sexy as hell.

"Oh, sometimes I come grocery shopping over here." She gestured at her cart, which held a lone frozen dinner. "I was on my way to the check-out line."

"You're only buying one thing?" I looked at my own overflowing basket.

She shrugged. "Well. I'm on a diet." More blushing.

Um. Okay.

"How's your running been? Get any long ones in since you rescued me on the towpath?"

"Nah. Been too damn busy. Hey, how's that ankle?" I looked down to see she was wearing some clunky platform-y things on her feet.

Her ankle looked pretty healthy.

"Oh, I got lucky. Really lucky. It didn't turn out to be much of a sprain at all, thank goodness. But I can't run for a couple weeks. Such a bummer."

She was a little odd. Or maybe eccentric was a better word. But something about her was making me crazy. Dammit.

And I knew I'd better not act on it.

Oh, how I longed for the days when I could pick up a hottie in the grocery store. But it was my dick that had gotten me into the trouble I was currently in, and I couldn't risk any more.

Such bullshit.

I found myself wanting to talk to her longer.

"So, what kind of work do you do, Cricket Curtain? By the way, that's a great name."

She rolled her eyes. "I don't know about it being a *great* name. More like a weird name. Real name is Christine."

Weird wasn't always a bad thing. Especially when you lived in the white bread world I did.

"I'm a, um, writer." She nodded, hesitating before saying more.

But that didn't stop me. "Writer? Cool. What kind of writer?"

She must have gotten that question all the time because she blurted out her answer before I'd even finished my question.

"Sad stuff. You know, about death and all."

"Oh. Interesting. Do you think I've read any of your stuff?" I asked.

That damn sexy blush washed over her face again. "Um. Probably."

Geez, she was a funny one. Hot, but funny. Which I had to admit, I was liking. A lot.

Down boy.

"Well," I said, "maybe I'll see you on the towpath."

She looked a tad disappointed.

Funny thing was, as I watched her walk away, she

limped slightly, favoring her right foot and leaning on her shopping cart in an effort to lessen the weight on it.

Hadn't it been the *left* ankle that she'd injured?

And who wears shoes like that when they have a hurt ankle?

Strange woman, that Cricket Curtain, but I got a kick out of her. It killed me to just let her walk away, regardless of which ankle she'd fucked up and that she'd strangely driven all way across town to buy one frozen dinner. I'd normally be all over a hottie like that, and in fact, my dick was getting hard just looking at her curvy ass.

But I had her name. I could find her if I had to.

It was just bad timing. But I knew things would improve.

They had to.

"Dad, good to see you," I said, shaking my old man's hand and joining him at the corner table of my favorite Indian restaurant.

"Good to see you, Son." He looked around the restaurant suspiciously and leaned closer. "You know, Indian food is fiery hot."

It had always been a challenge to get him to try what he and my mother referred to as 'ethnic food.'

"Dad, *some* Indian food is hot, not all of it. In fact, *most* of it is not."

He scanned the menu, unconvinced.

"I can help you choose some dishes," I said.

He sighed and closed his menu. "Yes. Do that, please."

I waved over the waitress and ordered two King-fisher beers.

"So, Dad, how are things?"

He looked around the restaurant to assess our privacy before he spoke, something he'd done for as long as I could remember.

I didn't like my personal information broadcast either, but I didn't go through life looking over my shoulder like he did.

He lowered his voice to where I could barely hear him. "You know, Son, this paternity thing should be over with soon."

God willing.

"You know something I don't?" I asked, tearing into a piece of naan bread.

Never one to show outward excitement, he took a slow sip of his beer. "My sources are close to proving that Carlotti was behind it all. We're working on solid proof."

I slammed my hand down on the table. "I *knew* it!"

All eyes in the restaurant turned my way before I even realized I'd made an outburst.

Whatever.

My dad ignored the explosion, but I had no doubt it irritated the shit out of him.

"Talbot, your mother and I were talking the other day."

Oh, shit. This did not bode well.

"We thought we'd encourage you to call Halliday Haynes. She's here in D.C., just like you are, and it seems like you have a lot in common."

Halliday Haynes. And old friend, Halliday was without a doubt one of the most beautiful women walking the face of the Earth. But she was also into older, rich men.

Which was fine with me. We were buddies. Always would be. I adored her and she adored me.

But dating? Hell, no.

That part my dad didn't know. But I would humor the man.

"What do you mean *call* her? Like ask her out on a date?"

My father pressed his lips together at my frankness. He was old school and had perfected indirectness to a fine art.

"Yes, Talbot. We are suggesting you see her socially. You can call it a *date* if you want."

What Dad didn't know—and neither did Halliday's parents, who were friends with *my* parents—was that she was, on occasion, my plus one to events, and I returned the favor when she couldn't be seen with her *real* partner. Which was pretty much all the time.

Halliday's man of the moment was one of Washington's highest-ranking officials—a married man with four kids—so mum was the word on her being his mistress. Although, I suspected a lot of people knew, anyway.

They just didn't talk about it. But they sure did *whisper* about it. That's how Washington worked.

So, neither my nor Halliday's parents knew a thing about her love life, which wasn't a problem until someone decided to play matchmaker.

Like now.

"I'll give that some consideration, Dad."

No point in arguing.

"I mean, she's a beautiful woman, and we *are* friends," I said, throwing him a bone.

A smile crept across his face, the first I'd seen that evening. I felt a little shitty for giving him false hope.

My parents would love nothing more than to see me partner off with Halliday Haynes. She was from *our world*, as my mother liked to say. Across-the-board privilege.

Which made Halliday and me laugh our asses off. The pretense would be tragic if it weren't so funny.

"Very well, Talbot. Your mother and I think this could be good for you."

Right. They'd thought becoming a senator would be good for me, too.

CHAPTER SEVEN

CRICKET

"Over here!"

In the noise and confusion at the arrivals curb at Providence's Green International Airport, I spotted my mom waving frantically.

She gestured to hurry as a parking enforcement officer drove up behind her old Honda Accord.

Seriously? They weren't even giving me a moment to get in the car?

So, I hustled, and Mom peeled out just as I pulled the door shut, leaving the officer to find someone else to scold.

"Jesus, could they make it any harder to get in and out of airports?" She sighed. "Good to see you, Cricket. I'm happy to have you home for the weekend."

She squeezed my hand. She could be so nice.

Louise Curtain was a good mom. Sometimes, even better than good, but I'm not sure I would go as far as saying she was great. I had friends who called their moms their *best friends*. I was not one of those people. I wished I were. I'd always been envious of women who had moms who stuck by them through thick and thin and were their biggest cheerleaders. My mom meant well, so there was that. But we were so different.

At one time, I'd been on track for a life like my mother's—marry young, have a kid or two, stay in Rhode Island all my life. But that changed when I was in high school. She and I hadn't seen eye to eye since.

Like most teenagers, my friends and I suffered interminable boredom, and we weren't always smart about how we spent our time.

One morning, I got to school to find gossip spreading like wildfire. Some kids were in tears, and some were strangely gleeful to have juicy news to gab about.

I cornered the most reliable girl I knew, and asked her if it was true.

Two girls from our class had been in a car crash the night before. One had died, and the other had a permanent brain injury.

They'd been my friends.

I'd almost hung out with them that night but had missed their call.

I could have been in that car.

It had been a night like many others. The girls had

each swiped some beer from their parents' stash, and had driven around the backroads of Rhode Island, drinking and laughing until they failed to stop at a rural four-way stop.

The woman in the car they hit had died, too.

I wandered in and out of my classes like a zombie that day. I didn't speak a word and spent my lunch sitting outside on the bleachers while a couple kids from the track team ran laps.

I cut out for the day before my last class. No one said a thing.

And now, as my mother and I drove by my old high school, I remembered vividly how, in my numbness, the early autumn sun had felt on my face that lunch hour, and how the weeds growing through the cracks of the poorly maintained track stood against the breeze. As I'd watched them bear the harsh conditions they were subjected to, like being regularly trampled on by the track team, I'd had an epiphany of sorts. At least, as much of an epiphany as you can have when you're sixteen years old.

I was getting the hell out of that town. It's not that it was a bad place, but I had to go somewhere where there was more to do than drink and drive. My friends had wasted their lives, and I'd make up for what they were going to miss. I didn't know how I'd do it, but I would.

After the accident, I'd hunkered down, gotten straight A's, and mostly kept to myself.

When we'd arrived at my mother's house, I sent Bridget a text to come get me in an hour. My mom and I would have a cup of tea like we always did, and then Bridget and I would head to nearby Newport, just like old times.

"What kind of tea would you like, honey? The usual?"

"That would be great, Mom," I called as I dumped my things in her basement guest room.

We settled into her living room, and I watched the steam rise from my cup. It felt good in the cooler Rhode Island temperature.

"So, how's work?"

I knew that was coming, but she was so damn sincere, I played along.

"I'm still in obits, Mom," I said with a big sigh. "But I'm trying to get out. Hoping for an interview with the new senator from New York. We went to college together."

She frowned, then recognition crossed her face. "Is he the one who—"

I nodded. "Yeah. He's embroiled in a big controversy."

"Well. Watch out for him," she said, shaking her head.

I was going to respond until I thought the better of it. Why bother?

"You know, if D.C. is not working out, you can always come home... "

Here we go...

"...and get a job at the paper in Providence. You could live with me while you're looking for a place of your own. It would be so nice to have you back here, and I know it would make Bridget real happy, too."

"Yeah, Mom, I'll probably stay in D.C."

As if I hadn't just said a thing, she continued, "You spent all that money on that fancy private university, and look how far it's gotten you."

Time to hit the road.

It had been a disappointment of massive proportion that my mother, however well meaning, had never supported my interest in getting an education, much less the expensive one I'd finagled. But every time it started to get me down, I thought of how much I'd accomplished without her support—things I'd done with sheer will. I had a job at a prestigious paper, and while it wasn't the work I wanted to do forever, I couldn't completely knock it. And, I had a decent-enough little apartment where, if you craned your neck just so, you could get a glimpse of the Potomac River.

I downed my tea before wasting my breath convincing her I was on the right track and wasn't a huge fuck up. "I think I hear Bridget. We're going to Newport for lunch at Brick Alley. See you later!"

I bolted out the door just as she pulled up.

"Oh, my god. We so need to get out of here," I said, hopping in.

She turned the car around and we hit the road. "Uh-oh. Mom getting under your skin?"

I looked over at my best friend. "Same old story. She thinks I was silly to *pay all that money for that fancy school.*"

I looked out the window and watched several ugly strip malls whiz by. I couldn't wait to get to Newport, to smell the salt air and enjoy the town's charm.

"I had an idea for before we go to Newport," Bridget said.

"Really? Usually, you can't get there fast enough."

She laughed. "I know. But I have a short detour."

We pulled into a gravel parking lot, greeted by a sign that said 'Simmons Farm.' I'd been by the place before, but had never given it any thought, figuring it was like all the other farms in Rhode Island.

"What are we doing here?" I asked.

She hopped out of the car and hustled toward a barn. "C'mon. Hurry up."

I ran to catch up, while Bridget paid a five-dollar admission for us each.

What were we being admitted to?

I followed to the doorway of a tiny barn, and as my eyes adjusted to the dim light, I realized it was full of baby goats and a few hens clucking over in a corner. Some of the little ones were sleeping, some were checking us out, and one dashed up to me and began to chew on my shoes.

A young woman in denim overalls appeared at my side. "You can pick her up. She loves being handled."

When she saw me hesitate, she scooped up the little bugger and thrust her into my arms.

Was I in the *Twilight Zone* or something?

Not five minutes before, I was fending off my mother's insinuations that I wasted money going to college, and lamenting whether I'd ever have a real career at the Washington Chronicle. Now, I was in farm heaven.

And not just farm heaven, but baby goat heaven.

"Her name is Sally," the farmhand said.

Now that my feet were out of reach of Sally's mouth, she craned her little neck over my shoulder to chew my hair.

I couldn't help but laugh.

"Isn't this place magical?" Bridget said. "I bring Brandon and the twins here every now and then. Even Simon likes it."

She was right. It *was* magical. Holding a squirming baby goat, not to mention trying to keep my long hair out of its mouth, was a distraction from all that was stressful in my life. I could have stayed there all day.

Maybe even for the rest of my life.

Could I actually be a... farmhand?

Yeah, right.

Bridget had corralled a fat red hen into her arms and brought it over to me. "Feel how soft her feathers are."

Just as I reached to stroke her, the goat bleated, startling the hen. Alarmed, the hen reached to peck at the goat, which successfully dodged her, leaving my arm to catch the brunt of her peck. It hurt like hell, and blood began to well where the skin was broken.

The farmhand came running over and took the chicken from Bridget.

"Bad girl," she scolded the hen.

"Didn't realize this was a blood sport." I set the goat down, and she returned to chewing on my shoes.

"Miss, you should clean that really well. Chickens carry salmonella, you know."

Great.

I'd officially had enough of farm life.

On the way back to the car, Bridget held pressure on my bleeding arm.

Guess I was lucky my best friend was a nurse.

She lifted the tissue she'd put on my arm and saw it was still oozing blood. "You know, I really think you need a tetanus shot, and maybe even a stitch. That little bugger took a small but deep chunk out of your arm."

Seriously?

"Let's go to the hospital. We'll have Simon take a look."

I looked around the bucolic farm. It had all seemed so harmless.

"But what about lunch?" I whined.

∾

"Well, if it isn't the lovely Washington, D.C. journalist, gracing us with a visit," Simon said in a curtained-off hospital treatment room, giving me that European double kiss that had enchanted us all the moment we'd met him.

I tried not to crush on Bridget's guy, but it was hard. Damn hard.

But she knew. I'd told her. I think every one of our girl friends had confessed the same to her. And she loved it.

Simon examined my tiny injury. "Well, love, you're not going to bleed to death, but chickens are not known to be particularly clean. Let's start with a tetanus shot. Pull down your pants."

"*What?*" Alarmed, I looked at Bridget, who started laughing.

"You don't have to pull them all the way. Just enough so he can get to your hip."

Simon waved around a long hypodermic needle. "Or you can pull them down all the way. It's no secret I'm an ass man."

Bridget play-slapped him on the arm. "For heaven's sake."

"Ouch!" I cried at the shot. "That hurt like hell."

Simon nodded. "Good. That means we got the muscle."

Easy for him to say. I wasn't going to be able to sit on that butt cheek for the rest of the day.

Then Simon focused on my arm, flushing it with

some liquid. "You don't need stitches but keep this clean."

When he was done, he leaned over and gave his wife a peck on the lips.

He was wild about her.

"Glad you're coming to Block Island with us. It'll be awesome. Wait 'til you see the house we've rented. Hey, are you bringing a plus-one?"

I shook my head as I rubbed my sore, bandaged arm. "Nah. Unless you have any hot friends to bring over from the U.K."

"You're not finding any interesting guys down there in D.C.?" he asked.

"Not to date. There is one guy, a young senator, who I'm trying to get an interview with. He's the embodiment of handsomeness. But he's not a potential date."

Bridget frowned. "You keep saying that. Why not?"

"Oh, guys like that date socialites and such. Not working girls like me."

Simon rolled his eyes. "Well, he should have his head examined if he's passing up a woman like you. Any man in the U.K. would give his eye teeth for a babe like you." He looked me up and down and growled.

I burst out laughing. "Okay, Simon. If you say so. I'll get a ticket to the U.K. today. I may never return."

"Well, I don't know what's wrong with American guys. They've got their heads up their arses, if you ask me."

Bridget kissed him again. "See you for dinner, darling."

Simon was one of the good ones, as they say, and I was infinitely happy he and Bridget had found each other. Something to strive for.

No doubt about it.

Simon had planted a seed, so as soon as I was back in D.C., I reactivated my Match.com account.

I'd been on it before, a couple years earlier, and let's just say, I was underwhelmed. But it was always possible that the dating pool had dramatically improved in the last two years.

Yeah, right.

So, I placed my ad along with a pretty decent photo and waited for the responses to roll in. I knew better than to get my hopes up, and boy, was I right.

Not much had changed in the two years since I'd last been on the site.

First came the dick pics. Small, big, erect, limp—I got them all. Some were completely shaved of pubic hair, and some protruded like little nubs in a hair sweater. I hadn't really been aware of all the variety among penises until these men indulged me.

None of the dicks were accompanied by faces.

Then I got the show-offs and guys trying to impress. There were pics of them in their expensive and not-so-expensive cars, in front of iconic sites like the Taj Mahal and the Great Wall of China, and even some at their desks in their oh-so-impressive Washington, D.C. jobs.

There was one, however, who stood out among the fray. That wasn't saying much, but I decided to give him a shot.

And that turned out to be a mistake.

I showed up at The Tombs on 36ᵗʰ Street, a hip dive bar sort of place that had been around forever. Across the dark room, someone stood and waved, presumably my date, who was a medical resident at Georgetown University Hospital.

"You must be Cricket," he said, extending his hand. "I'm Harry."

So far, so good. Decent manners.

"Whew, what a day I had." He mimed wiping his brow and gestured for the waiter.

I was about to ask for a chardonnay, when Harry interrupted, "I need another beer please. Stat."

Did he think he was still at the hospital?

Turning toward me, he dismissed the waiter, who took off running.

So much for my chardonnay.

"Well, Cricket, you are very pretty, just like your photo. I tell you, the majority of women on Match are *not as advertised*." He used air quotes for emphasis.

"Yes, I guess that goes both ways—"

Interrupted again.

"I mean, most of them are way *older* than they list in

their ads, and they're nearly all way *fatter*, too." He leaned back in his chair as if he'd been mortally insulted, and shook his finger at me.

"What is it with women? They're such goddamn liars."

Okayyy...

"Cricket, you would not believe my day."

Now that my eyes were adjusted to the light, I could see he still wore his hospital ID, hanging big and obvious from his shirt pocket.

Dork alert.

The waiter returned with a beer, which Harry took a big swig of.

"Excuse me," I said after the departing waiter, "I'd like to order please."

He came hustling back. "Right. What would you like?"

As soon as the waiter was gone, Harry continued, "I'm doing my surgical rotation now, as you probably know—"

I didn't know, but good information to have, should I need surgery.

"—and today, I removed breasts from no fewer than three women with cancer."

He sat back, smiling proudly. I had the feeling that if he were in private, he'd be beating his chest.

A bile taste grew in my mouth.

What. A. Dick.

The waiter returned with my wine and plopped a

bill down next to me. When I looked at him with a shocked expression, he said, "Um, well, your friend here asked for separate checks."

"Oh. Okay." I handed the waiter a twenty.

"Or, you can give him your card and start a tab like I did, if you think you're going to be here for a while."

Fat fucking chance of that.

"Would you like to know what I'm doing tomorrow at the hospital—"

I took a big sip of my wine and stood. "Harry, could you excuse me while I go to the ladies' room?"

"Oh, sure. Yeah. Take your time. I'm ordering another beer."

Choke on it, buddy.

I headed straight for the door and didn't look back.

The waiter could keep my twenty for having to deal with that douche bag.

The next day, I headed straight for DogHouse after work. Even though a chicken had tried to maul me the previous weekend, I was desperate for some animal time. Walking puppies would take my mind off the disappointment that had been Harry the Bad Date who bragged about his surgical prowess.

I got my little pups all leashed up, and we started down the sidewalk. The buggers ran in every direction, not yet socialized to the concept of walking in a straight line. It took a lot of concentration to make sure none of them ate rocks or worse, but when I looked up, I could swear I saw Talbot Richardson march into the community center a couple doors down.

What the hell was he doing at the community center?

I approached the door, and since it was wide open, I slipped in, hoping I wouldn't be chased out because of the dogs.

"May I help you, Miss?" an elderly lady asked.

"Oh, I'm looking for a friend."

"Okay, then." She smiled at the dogs and walked away.

I wandered toward a massive gym, and a minute later, Talbot appeared, having changed into gym clothes. He shook a bunch of balls out of a net bag and started throwing them to the dozen or so kids surrounding him.

"Yo, Mister Senator Man, toss me one," a short, loud kid shouted.

Talbot laughed and tossed a ball over. He started issuing instructions to his charges and then spotted me.

A puzzled look, then recognition crossed his face. He waved, said something to the kids, and started walking toward me.

Holy shit. He was a coach there?

"Well, what a surprise," he said, hands on hips, and looking incredibly hot in his basketball shorts and community center T-shirt. "And look at these puppies."

"Yeah, what a surprise, no kidding. How are you? I heard the kids call you Senator."

As if I didn't know...

He bent down to scratch one of the pups behind the ears, and it jumped up and kissed him on the mouth.

Kind of like I wanted to.

He looked back up at me. "Yeah. About the senator thing..."

CHAPTER EIGHT

TALBOT

I had to say hello when I spotted jogging-girl-who-might-not-really-have-had-a-sprained-ankle, also known as Cricket Curtain.

Of all places, she was in the community center where I coached kids' basketball.

With several unruly puppies on leashes.

I couldn't really say it was surprising, seeing her there. I'd already run into her on the towpath and in the grocery store. Who knew where she'd turn up next?

But it wasn't just the puppies that drew me to her that day, even though they were hilariously running in every direction, tangling her legs in their leashes. It wasn't just that she was desperately trying to corral them with a soft voice and patience I'd never have.

Nor was it the floaty little dress she was wearing that showed off her legs for miles.

No.

It was the look in her eyes of sheer surprise when she saw me on the basketball court with a bunch of ten-year-old boys jumping up and down like little wild men, making enough noise to drown out a freight train.

She *got* it.

I knew I'd never have to explain to her why volunteering with a bunch of rambunctious kids was the happiest part of my day.

"...to answer your question, I'm the new senator from New York. And I might ask you, what are you doing with these puppies?"

Her face brightened, kind of the way mine did when I talked about my basketball kids.

"I'm a puppy walker. DogHouse, the puppy rescue agency, is just two doors down. I thought I saw you and was wondering if my eyes were playing tricks on me."

"What? You didn't think I'd volunteer at a community center?" I asked.

She cocked her head, choosing her words carefully. "No, it's not that. I would have figured you'd be so busy, just having moved back to D.C."

I was about to ask about her ankle, but my mini ball players interrupted, shouting across the gym. "Ooooh, look at Mister Senator Man, talking to that pretty girl!"

I turned to find that Cricket and I had an audience

and were on the receiving end of a mountain of ten-year-old speculation.

The kids were laughing and elbowing each other, enjoying my meeting with Cricket as much as I was.

"C'mon guys, get back to your drills." I tried to wave them away but only succeeded in encouraging more jeering.

"Is that your girlfriend or your sister, Mister Senator Man?"

"It's his wife!"

"Naw, nobody that pretty would marry his skinny butt."

That threw them all into hysterics, and I caught Cricket trying to stifle a laugh, too. Pretty soon, we were both shaking with laughter. As soon as I could compose myself, I turned to my hecklers.

"I'll cancel today's practice if you guys don't get to work. NOW!"

That shut them down, and they began frantically running the court as I'd instructed.

"Punks," I said, when I turned back to Cricket.

"I am just speechless," she said, her still trying not to laugh.

"They're funny as hell, aren't they?" I loved those kids.

She shook her head. "They don't care one bit who you are. They are completely unimpressed."

I knew she'd get it.

I looked back at them, then at Cricket's puppies, one of which had just piddled on the floor.

"I'll tell you what. Finish your dog walking, and then meet me here. I want to take you to coffee."

A pink tinge spread across her face that was so fucking cute, a little twitch below the belt reminded me I hadn't talked to someone I was attracted to in quite some time.

Down boy.

I found myself seriously hoping she was free. I needed to spend some time with someone outside of politics. And, it didn't hurt that she was hot as hell, and was into volunteering.

She bit her lower lip and looked at her watch. "All right. I'll be done in about an hour, if that works for you."

Even though the kids were spying on my every move and I should have pretended to be indifferent, I couldn't help but watch her walk away, her red hair blowing in the evening breeze and her skirt swinging around her great legs.

I got back to the kids. We were all going to get a hard workout over the next hour... because that's just what I was in the mood for.

~

As we were winding down, I looked up to see Cricket waiting in the stands for me.

I blew my whistle to end practice and got the rowdiest two kids to pick up all the balls and return them to the storage closet.

"Hey," I said to her, "I'm gonna grab a quick shower."

Damn if she didn't give me that dazzling smile again. "Sure. Take your time. I have a book I can read here on my phone."

She was a reader. *Yes.*

While I took my shower, keeping an eye on the boys who were, as always, raising hell in the locker room, I thought back to how Cricket and I had overlapped at college for a couple years. I wracked my brain but could not, for the life of me, remember any redheads.

It was bizarre. I'd always had a thing for redheads. How could I have missed her?

Had I had my head that far up my ass?

When I'd finally herded all the kids out of the locker room to catch their rides home, I returned to the gym where I found Cricket talking to Mrs. Herman, the elderly woman who worked the center's front desk.

"Ladies, hope I'm not interrupting anything," I said when they stopped talking and looked at me.

"Oh, say, Senator, we wanted to know if you'll be continuing with your coaching? We're putting together next month's schedule."

"Mrs. Herman, call me Talbot. Or Tal. You don't have to call me Senator. In fact, I would rather you not call me that."

She giggled and looked at Cricket, then looked back at me.

"Hey, do you two know each other? Because if you don't, you should," she said slyly.

So, Mrs. Herman was a matchmaker. She had damn good taste.

Cricket straightened. "We already know each other, if you can believe it. We went to the same college."

Mrs. Herman's eyes brightened, and a naughty smile crept across her face.

"To answer your question, Mrs. Herman, yes, I am continuing with my volunteering. Sometimes I think it's the only thing that keeps me sane," I said.

"Okay then. I'll put you on the schedule. The kids will be thrilled. Well, so will all the moms too, if ya know what I mean."

She walked away, chuckling at her own joke.

"Must be hell being a sex symbol," Cricket said as we headed out.

I rolled my eyes at her. "Funny girl."

~

We walked over to Union Station to a little coffee place I liked. Turned out it was packed, and the only seat was a small bench in the window where we had to sit side by side. Very closely.

No complaints from me. Cricket's leg rubbed against mine, and as it did, the hem of her skirt inched a little higher. I could barely keep my gaze off her smooth skin and the downy hair covering it.

Christ, I was a fucking perv.

And I loved it.

"So, what's up with the puppy walking?"

The best thing about sitting so close was her damn scent. I didn't know if it was her shampoo or what, but it was plain and clean. And damn sexy.

Her face lit up again. "DogHouse is my sanity check, kind of like the basketball coaching is for you. I live for my visits with the puppies. Sometimes, it's the highlight of my day." She shook her head and laughed. "God, that sounds pathetic, doesn't it?"

I winked at her. "Just a little."

And she nudged me hard in the ribs.

"I'd really like to have a dog, but they aren't permitted in my apartment. So, I get my fix at the puppy rescue. It's an awesome place. They do so much good there."

God, it was sweet how she lit up, talking about the dogs.

"I got into volunteering when I was growing up in Rhode Island. I taught reading to kids with developmental disabilities. But Rhode Island got a bit small for me. I always wanted to come to D.C. So, I leveraged my future and took on a bunch of debt to go to GW."

She changed the subject. "How'd you end up in the Senate? Had you always wanted to be a politician? I don't remember you running for anything in college."

I took a deep breath. "No. I'd not really wanted to be a politician."

Shit, did I say that too loudly? I looked around but found no one was paying any attention to us.

"To be honest, my parents pushed me into it. My dad was a senator, and he had the political machine all set up. He had contacts and knew how to raise money—all he needed was a candidate. That's where I came in."

Fuck, I couldn't believe I'd just shared that with someone I barely knew. But strangely, I was comfortable telling her things I wouldn't breathe to most.

She studied me, obviously curious about my take on where I'd ended up in life. "Sounds like you entered politics kicking and screaming."

Christ, was it that easy to see? And if so, how the hell did I fool the voters of New York?

"What I really wanted to do was go into the Peace Corps. That was my dream.."

And it was feeling further and further away every day.

She tilted her head at me. "Really?"

"I mean, don't get me wrong. I feel very fortunate to have been elected to the Senate. It will be a great six years, maybe more if I run for reelection. The Peace Corps can wait."

"I see."

"Hey, you gotta keep that under wraps, okay? If the public knew my real passion, I'd be fucked. And my dad would blow his top."

I glanced at my watch and realized I needed to head out, much as I hated to leave the lovely Cricket. I was facing another ass-crack-of-dawn meeting with some committee members.

"Can I see you to your car?" I asked.

"Sure," she said.

We walked in silence for a minute, but I had the distinct feeling she wanted to tell me something.

Turned out, I was right.

"Hey, you might not know this, but I work for the Washington Chronicle," she said, looking up at me and smiling.

Shit. Had I just poured my heart out only to have it show up on the front page of the paper the next morning? I mean, she'd told me she was a writer, but not a writer for a huge goddamn newspaper.

I needed to learn to keep my big fucking mouth shut.

"What do you do for the paper?"

"I write the obituaries."

Ohthankgod.

"No shit. What's that like?"

She shrugged. "It's a good place to start at the paper. Don't get me wrong. I feel very fortunate to have my job. But I hope to work on real news at some point."

By the time we'd reached her car, I was dying to kiss her.

But she took a deep breath and kept talking. "You know, I'd really like to do an interview of you, as the youngest senator ever elected, and having come through such a difficult race."

Well, shit.

"Cricket, you probably know that I'm in a difficult situation right now with a paternity suit."

She nodded. "Yes, I am aware of that. Sounds like a terrible thing to go through."

"On the advice of my attorney, I can't talk to the press until we get the DNA results. I'm on an interview moratorium."

Disappointment crossed her face before she could replace it with an understanding smile. "Yeah. I know. I just thought it wouldn't hurt to ask."

I moved closer to her, feeling a bit badly for turning her down, but overwhelmed with a need to kiss her. I backed her up against her car door and wove my fingers into that thick, red hair.

Running my lips down her temple, I inhaled the scent of her hair again. Pausing, I kissed her ear and continued to her lips. They were soft and relaxed, and her eyes fluttered closed when our mouths met.

Fuck. It was like fireworks went off. Something about this woman slayed me. She was scrappy and down to earth—I'd not known many women like that. And I wanted to know more.

"Cricket Curtain," I whispered into her mouth.

"Mmmm..."

"Funny name."

She pulled back and smiled. "You trying to pick a fight?"

After we laughed, our mouths crashed together again, and this time, I parted her lips with my tongue. She was sweet, just like I knew she'd be, and I let my hands wander down her back until I had handfuls of her curvy ass.

Christ, I wanted to take her home.

But the timing wasn't right. I wasn't the most patient man, but I also knew not to fuck up a good thing.

"When can I see you again, Cricket Curtain?"

She looked surprised. Maybe she often kissed guys and never saw them again?

"Well, soon, I hope," she murmured, pressing tightly against me.

There was no doubt she felt my raging hard-on because she took the opportunity to grind her sexy hips right into it.

If I didn't watch it, I'd explode in my pants right there.

But she stopped before I did and pulled the car door open.

"Have a good night." She winked at me, hopped into her car, and peeled out of the parking lot.

Yeah, thanks. I'd have a great night, just me and my blue balls.

CHAPTER NINE

CRICKET

S o close.
　　And yet...

Fuck, Fuck. Fuckity fuck.

I mean, Talbot was gorgeous, athletic, and he coached kids' basketball.

And he'd kissed me.

So there was that.

But I wasn't any closer to getting a story on him than I'd been when I'd embarked on my mission, starting on the Georgetown towpath, faking a sprained ankle.

I couldn't complain about the kiss, though. All was not *completely* lost.

What was I going to tell Ken, my editor in chief? *Sorry, Ken. Can't deliver. Just keep me in obits for my entire career like my quirky boss Wayne. Maybe I'll end up going to funerals for fun just like he does.*

I'd foolishly thought I'd get ahead on merit. Get your ass to work everyday, don't make any trouble, and work your ass off. Be a good girl.

Why did figuring this shit out come so hard to me? Other people seemed to know how to maneuver through life just on instinct.

I'd finally gotten the message—loud and clear, I might add—that what really propelled a career was *who* you knew. Just like the old saying.

So, I dug myself into a hole by bragging about being buds with Talbot.

Look at me! I know someone!

A lot of good all that lying did me. It got me an assignment I couldn't deliver on.

Why had Ken wanted *me* to do this story, anyway? I mean, with all his Washington connections, he probably could have made a couple phone calls and gotten an interview in minutes.

Was this a set-up? Some sort of test?

Of course it was. Just like the rest of my life. Could I get out of Rhode Island, get an expensive college education, and make it in Washington, D.C.?

With quite a bit of effort, I'd managed the first two. But the last? Make it in Washington, D.C.?

I just couldn't get my career off the ground. Maybe my mom had been right. Come home. Get a job at a small, local paper. But *throw in the towel* was what she'd really meant. My big ambitions were unseemly for a girl with such humble beginnings. She'd never said that, of course, but I knew that's what she thought.

"Hi, Ken. You wanted to see me?" I stood in the doorway of his office, praying he didn't really need me and that the IM he'd sent requesting that I join him in his office was meant for someone else.

Seriously?

"Cricket! Come on in. Take a seat."

He leaned onto his desk and smiled like we were old friends.

"So, what have you got for me?" He rubbed his hands together.

Ugh. Just what I've been dreading.

So, I decided to tell the truth.

"I approached Talbot, and he told me he's on an interview moratorium, which I expected. I plan to see him again soon, though, to keep working on him."

I left out the kissing part.

Ken clapped his hands together and popped to his feet. "That's great news! I knew you could do it."

He did?

Grabbing his suit coat from behind his office door, he said, "I'm off to have lunch with the ambassador from the Great Britain so I'll see you later. Keep up the good work."

And he was gone.

Wow. I still had a chance. Ken didn't think I was a total loser. Yet.

As soon as I was back in my cluttered cube, Wayne wandered over.

"Hey, Cricket, what did Ken want?"

So nosy. But then again, he *was* my boss.

"He wanted to know if I'd made any progress on the Richardson story."

Wayne smirked. "I don't know how you're supposed to do that when you have over a dozen obits to do today."

Creep.

"I know, right? I'd better get jamming, then." I turned back to my computer and began typing in the hope that he'd just disappear.

What he didn't know was that I could finish all my work in about two hours. So, I took the opportunity to visit my favorite Facebook group for puppy videos. When I'd exhausted their new ones, I turned to the news.

And don't you know, first thing to pop up in my feed was the young and handsome Senator Talbot Richardson.

The one I'd just had coffee with. And kissed.

And he wasn't alone.

No, he was in the company of a stunning brunette who smiled like she was born for the limelight.

Seriously. They looked so good together I wanted to send them a wedding present.

While I hadn't placed a huge amount of stock in the fact that Talbot had kissed me and asked me out for a future date, my heart still felt like a balloon that someone had unkindly stuck a pin into.

Well, shit.

Apparently, they'd been to some charity tennis event and were leaving arm and arm, all smiles, probably to go home and fuck like rabbits.

Whatever.

I'd barely processed the unexpected disappointment of seeing Talbot with a beauty worthy of Miss America, when a text from him popped up on my phone.

Great. A real player.

Didn't the fool know there were photos of him online with a woman who appeared to be very fond of him?

So, I ignored the text and continued writing up the obituary of the creator of a popular children's TV show.

Not five minutes later, my phone buzzed again.

I was about to ignore it again, when I realized I needed to swallow my pride and continue to try to get an interview with this guy.

do you have a second to talk?

sure

Not ten seconds later, my cell rang.

"Hello," I said with the flattest voice I could muster.

"Hey Cricket."

Why was I thinking back to our kiss, how slow, delicious, and sexy it was? Dammit.

"Hey Talbot. What's up?"

I was the queen of indifference.

"I have an event coming up, a formal ball, and I wanted to invite you."

Why didn't he invite the hot babe on his arm in today's news?

Be nice.

"Thank you for thinking of me. But aren't you dating someone?"

Why couldn't I get the image of his thick dark hair, strong jaw, and mesmerizing blue eyes out of my mind?

He chuckled. "What makes you think that?"

Since my truth telling was on a roll, I decided to stick with it.

"A photo of you popped up my news feed today and showed you with a woman. I just figured you guys were dating."

He was silent for a moment. "Hmmm. What did she look like?"

Shit, he dated so many women he couldn't remember them? No wonder he was tagged with a paternity suit.

"Um, long brown hair, tall. Very beautiful. The caption said it was from a charity event or something like that."

Hopefully, he couldn't tell I'd studied the photo for a

full fifteen minutes and re-read the caption no less than five times.

"Oh, that was Halliday. Halliday Haynes. She's just a friend. An old friend."

Um, yeah.

"We are occasionally each other's plus-one. I grew up with her—she's my buddy from way back. Like a sister, really." Then, he lowered his voice. "She actually sees a married man, but that's totally on the down-low. She hides it by being seen with me and other guy friends."

Oh. Well.

"Our parents don't know. Nobody does. In fact, my dad keeps bugging me to ask her out. He has no idea that I'm the last guy she'd be interested in. She likes 'em older. You know, the silver fox type."

"Well, okay. I guess I can go."

"Don't sound so excited. Okay, look, it's Friday night. I'll pick you up at six. It's black tie."

Our called ended with my previously balloon-pricked heart re-inflating with the excitement of spending time with a gorgeous man, who also had the heart of a volunteer. *That* was hot.

What wasn't so hot was that I had two days to get ready for a ball. A freaking *ball*.

Maybe some people had the ball thing under control. Like, they went to them all the time, knew what to wear, how to act, and how to prepare.

Me? I knew how to get ready to go out for coffee, and that was about it.

So I turned to my source of all things Washington.

I picked up my phone and began to frantically text my work buddy.

aimee. are you at your desk

yeah. what's up

emergency! can you come to my cube

OMW

She must have sprinted across the office, no easy feat in the high heels she wore.

"What the hell, Cricket?"

I looked over my cube wall to make sure no one could hear us.

"Remember that senator I was supposed to write a story about?"

She nodded. "Yeah. How's that coming?"

"It's not. But listen. He invited me to a ball. Like a black tie ball. For this Friday."

Her mouth dropped open. "No shit!"

"I know, right? I can't believe it either. Don't tell anyone here at work. I said yes, but I probably shouldn't have."

She frowned. "Why? Why the hell not?"

I sighed in exasperation. Was she for real?

"I wouldn't know where to start to get ready for a ball. I don't have anything to wear, I don't know how to do my hair, *and* there's no way I can lose the extra seven pounds I've been carrying by Friday." I threw my hands up in the air.

"Okay, first of all, stop whining," she said, shaking a finger in my face. "Then, I'm going to tell you exactly what to do. You will follow my instructions, and you will be a hit. You got me?"

I knew Aimee would make it all better.

"Give me a piece of paper," she demanded. "After work, we're going to Second Hand Rose, the George-town consignment shop where all the rich ladies send their stuff. You'll probably have your choice of some great gowns. Then, I'm gonna call my hair guy for you. He knows how to handle fancy. And last, shut up about losing weight because you look amazing."

My eyes filled with tears and my voice choked. "I knew I could count on you."

~

If I ever had any doubts about Aimee's ability to deliver, they were now gone.

After shimmying into my second-hand gown, I turned in front of my Ikea full-length mirror in disbe-lief. If someone had shown me a picture of myself and sworn it was me, I'm pretty sure I'd have told them they were crazy.

True to her word, Aimee had found me an incredible deep blue evening gown that didn't need a stitch of alteration, for less than a hundred dollars. Even the length was perfect, which never happened. The dress was a strapless number, fitted in the bust, and flowing to the ground from its empire waistline, with a tiny train on the back.

It looked like something Jennifer Aniston would wear, the queen of minimalist elegance. And I was in love with it. Totally slimming and showed off the girls perfectly.

Her hairdresser had not disappointed, either. I'd told him I wanted something simple and not overly done. He blew out my hair, letting it drape softly around my shoulders, and placed some glittery barrette thing on the side. The contrast between my carrot top and the blue dress was amazing.

In short, I felt like the most beautiful girl in the world.

The hairdresser had someone at the salon do my make-up.

I was ready to attend my first Washington ball, on the arm of a gorgeous senator.

Suddenly, all my days spent in the disappointment of the obituary department were the furthest thing from my mind. I didn't have a care in the world. In fact, I was flying high above it. Rhode Island, and the accident of my high school years, stopped haunting me if only for a little while.

In order to buy myself some extra time for getting ready, I'd asked Talbot to meet me at the party rather than pick me up. He didn't seem too crazy about the idea, as if I was going to back out or something, but he'd agreed.

So now I could make an entrance, just like in the movies.

When I arrived, I texted Talbot, just as he'd asked.

I'm here

My heart was pounding in my chest. I'd plastered a bright smile on my face, and was sure to pull my shoulders back to show off my strapless dress to best advantage. If I could help it, no one would have any idea I was nervous. I scanned the crowd like I was some sort of superstar, the whole time trying not to trip on the hem of my dress.

When they said D.C. wasn't a stylish town, they only had it half right.

About fifty percent of the crowd were older ladies, many of whom looked like they were wearing dresses that dated back to the Reagan era. Big, poufy taffeta confections, with lots of lacquered, stiff hair.

The other half were the younger crowd, who looked like they might have raided Saks with their parents' credit cards. They were self-consciously chic, nervously looking around like little birdies to see which stars of Washington they could rub elbows with.

And it was amazing.

"Wow. Just wow," a male voice said in my ear.

I was tempted to whip around to see who it was but instead, I slowly turned, all fake composure.

As I'd hoped, it was Talbot. He leaned to kiss my

cheek, and I took his arm in an effort to seem friendly. In reality, I needed something to steady myself.

I'd known Talbot was hot since the beginning. And now, several years later, he was even more handsome. But I'd never seen him in black tie, and the way he looked at me, his gaze drilling into mine, took my freaking breath away.

I'd gotten what I had come for. I could die happy now.

He placed a gentle hand on my elbow. "Would you like some bubbly?"

What I really wanted was a big shot of tequila. But I was pretty sure I wasn't in the right place for that.

"Hey, there's my friend Halliday," he said, waving over the crowd at what must have been the most beautiful woman in the place.

She came rushing toward us.

"Oh my god, I can't believe all the assholes here." She wiped an invisible droplet of sweat off her brow.

"Halli, this is Cricket," Talbot said.

She turned to me with a huge smile and took my hands. "Cricket! Tal told me about you. And you're even more beautiful than he said."

Whoa.

We did the European double-cheek air kiss thing. "Great to meet you, Halli."

Would it be weird if I asked her to be my new best friend?

"And *you're* more beautiful than the picture in the news of you and Talbot."

She dropped her head back and poured forth the laugh of a beautiful, confident woman who didn't take the world too seriously.

I didn't know if things would go anywhere with Talbot, but this woman was awesome.

Talbot handed Halliday and me tall glasses of bubbly, and he sipped on some sort of brown liquor.

Scotch, I was guessing. Like all Masters of the Universe.

"So, you guys grew up together?" I asked.

She waved at someone across the room and nodded. "We did. Our parents are best friends. They'd love it if we got together, wouldn't they, Tal?" She looked at me and rolled her eyes.

He nodded. "They would, indeed. If only they knew your real proclivities."

She leaned toward him. "But they never will, right? Until I'm ready to tell them?"

Talbot ran a light finger across the bare skin of my shoulders, and I shivered at the sensation.

"Halli, your secret is safe with me. I don't *out* anybody," he said.

She pressed her forehead against his. "That's why I love you, little brother."

"Senator! So good to see you tonight."

Talbot turned to face an older gentleman, who began speaking to Talbot in a low voice.

Halliday nudged me. "C'mon. They have to do their power broker thing. Let's walk around."

Wow. This cool chick actually wanted to hang with me?

She lowered her voice. "Listen, I don't know if you come to these things often or what. If not, just be aware, they are full of cunty bitches. Be careful what you say to them, and trust no one. They'll stab you in the back as easily as they make appointments for their Botox injections."

"Um, okay. Thanks for the heads up." I didn't know what else to say. I mean, I knew I wasn't exactly with my typical people, but I hadn't realized danger lurked around every corner.

"Why do you come, then?"

I was dying to know.

"I have to. Everyone has to." She looked around the room. "I bet half the people here tonight would rather be at home watching Netflix. Personally, I'd rather be fucking John, but he's over there with his wife."

She turned up her nose.

Okay. The social rules of this world were about as foreign to me as brain surgery. I was clearly outmatched. I gazed around the room, still smiling and holding my head high, like someone was going to come after me with a box cutter at any second.

My stomach somersaulted for the third time that night. I didn't know how much more I could handle. I'd only had a handful of Triskets for dinner.

"Hey, I'm running to the ladies'."

She gulped the last of her champagne. "Okay. It's over that way," she said, gesturing.

Jesus, was there anything she didn't know about these parties?

In the bathroom stall, I gingerly lifted the hem of my dress and sat. I was scared to death of messing it up before the evening was out, so I was being extremely careful with the layered bottom of it.

It was good to have a second to myself, too.

The door to the ladies' room opened and closed. I decided to wait in my stall so I wouldn't have to make any more small talk than I absolutely had to.

"Jesus, did you see who he was with? I mean, one of the most eligible men in D.C. with someone like her?"

A tube of lipstick opened and closed, and then someone smacked her lips.

"I don't get it. Why the hell is he with such a rube? She looks like she walked out of the Miss America pageant with that silly dress. Which, by the way is from several seasons ago. Who wears dark blue for evening anymore?"

Holy fuck. They were talking about me, weren't they?

I didn't have to wait long to catch the wrath of the cunty bitches. Halliday hadn't been exaggerating.

"She's probably from his staff. We all know his reputation. I mean, look at the hot water he's in right now, with that paternity issue."

I was about to unlock the stall door and confront the bitches but thought better of it. Revenge is a dish best served cold, as they say.

I peeked through the crack in the stall door and saw they were two older ladies, whom I'd seen earlier in the evening.

I looked forward to meeting them again.

Soon.

CHAPTER TEN

TALBOT

I hadn't seen Cricket since Halliday had spirited her away, but I wasn't worried. I knew my old buddy would take care of my girl. Nevertheless, I didn't appreciate being monopolized by Senator Cazzo, an old fart politician and long-time acquaintance of my father's. He was old school, and instead of collaborating, he got his way with strong-arming threats.

Dude was going to learn the hard way that the younger generation didn't operate that way.

But I was saved from his smarminess when I was called to the stage to give my prepared remarks. I hadn't set eyes on Cricket in a while and scanned the crowd as I made my way through it.

"I'd like to thank everyone for coming tonight, and

for giving me the opportunity to make a few remarks about my new place in the U.S. Senate..."

I droned on with the requisite words that anyone at such an event would make and got off the stage as soon as I could.

And as luck would have it, the moment I did, I was cornered by Senator Cazzo's wife and some other matron of the Senate wives, most likely equally unpleasant.

Mrs. Cazzo squeezed my bicep, as if I were something she was considering taking home for dinner.

"Talbot," she purred, "I can call you Talbot, can't I? Or do you prefer Senator Richardson?"

She was a beautiful older woman, no doubt about it. The best plastic surgeons in D.C. had worked their magic on this old girl, and they'd done a damn good job. But for some reason, I wanted to take a shower after she ran her finger along my tux-covered arm.

"Talbot's fine, Mrs. Cazzo. I mean, we've known each other since my dad was in the Senate, and I was just a kid." I slipped my arm out of her reach.

I didn't mention that my father thought her husband was a lightweight blowhard who'd gotten by on his family fortune.

"Actually, Talbot, I think I've known you since you were in diapers." She turned to her friend, and they both laughed as if they'd seen me naked just last week.

And they were now completely creeping me out. I

looked through the crowd for Cricket. Where the hell had she gone?

"I only have a minute, Talbot," she said, lowering her voice, "but I wanted to tell you I'm not sure the woman you're with tonight is quite right for you."

Holy fuck. *That's* what this was about? Jesus, this woman was just as bad as her douchebag husband.

Her friend, whose name I still did not know, nodded gravely.

What a couple of bitches.

I cleared my throat in order to steady my voice. "What makes you say that, Mrs. Cazzo?"

Where in the *fuck* was Cricket? I knew how this crowd operated and was hoping someone hadn't eaten her alive.

Mrs. Cazzo smiled at me like I was the village idiot. "Look at you, sweetie. You are one of D.C.'s most eligible bachelors. You need to be with a woman of your caliber."

I needed to get the fuck away from these bitches. But not just yet.

"You're probably right, Mrs. Cazzo."

She looked at her buddy and smiled smugly.

I leaned closer to them. "The problem is, she sucks cock like a champ. I'm just not sure I can give that up."

The look on their faces was worth the price of admission.

I clapped my hands together. "You know what I mean?"

I finally spotted Cricket wandering around with a fresh glass of wine in her hand and waved her over.

"Baby, I've been looking for you." I threw an arm around her shoulder as she smiled sweetly for Mrs. Cazzo and her unnamed friend.

"Hello," she said, extending her hand, "I'm Cricket."

Just as the speechless Mrs. Cazzo extended her hand, someone behind us bumped into Cricket, sending her red wine flying down the front of the older woman's dress.

Mrs. Cazzo screamed.

"Oh, my god, let me get a napkin," her friend said, then disappeared into the crowd.

"My dress!"

Karma's a bitch, and all that.

"Oh, my goodness, I'm so sorry——"

But before Cricket could finish her apology, I steered her away from the vultures.

When we were a safe distance away from Mrs. Cazzo's wailing, I turned her to face me. "I was beginning to worry about you. Halliday take good care of you?"

She nodded. "She gave me fair warning."

I laughed. "The woman knows of what she speaks. She's been around this town for a while."

Cricket looked at me and winked.

No doubt, this girl was cool as shit.

"Hey, I haven't had the chance to tell you how fucking beautiful you are."

Seriously. Her strapless dress framed her luscious tits, almost offering them as a sexy little present that I was dying to run my lips over.

That, coupled with her loose, wavy red hair, ensured I needed to keep my tux jacket buttoned for fear of revealing my libidinous excitement.

Fucking hot, that's what she was. And modest, too.

"Thank you." She looked down for a moment, then back up at me.

I leaned my lips close to her ear and brushed them with a small kiss. Her eyes fluttered closed as her breath caught.

Exactly the reaction I'd been hoping for.

"Hey, did you spill your wine on purpose, or did someone really slam into you?"

She opened her eyes and tilted her head. "Wouldn't you like to know?"

This woman killed me.

"C'mon. We're getting out of here." I grabbed her hand and headed toward the door with my head down so I couldn't get pulled into any small talk.

She had to hustle to keep up with me.

"What about Halli? Shouldn't we say goodbye?"

"Nah, Halli will be fine. She probably knows more people here than I do. Plus, she likes to keep an eye on her man. He'll send his wife home later, and they'll fuck in the bathroom."

Cricket stopped in her tracks.

"Are you serious?"

I pulled her into a cab. "Serious as a heart attack, darlin'. This city might look conservative on the outside, but just behind the veneer of Brooks Brothers, these people are freaks."

As the cab sped across town, I lowered my lips to Cricket's and wrapped a hand under her delectable bottom.

"Fuck, baby, I'm dying to taste you," I whispered.

"Excuse me, sir, but where do you want to go?" the cabbie asked.

I threw several twenties over the seat at him. "Dude, just drive, okay?"

He sighed, scooping up the cash I'd given him, and looked straight ahead.

Cricket's mouth welcomed mine, and much to my delight, her hand reached right for my crotch.

That's what I'm talking about.

"Your hand feels good, baby, stroke that cock," I whispered.

She smiled against my lips and murmured, "Yeah, you like my hand on your big cock?"

Fuck. I almost blew my load right there.

"Yeah. But you know what I'd really like?" Now I was going to find out if I had a dirty girl on my hands. A man could always hope.

"You'd like my lips on your cock, I bet." She gripped me harder.

Bingo.

And wouldn't you know, the cab driver stole my little reverie right away. Cock-blocking bastard.

"Sir, I need to know where your destination is."

Shit. Couldn't blame the guy. He'd let us make out in his car long enough. Probably wanted to get rid of us before we got cum all over his seats.

I directed him to Cricket's place, and when we arrived, I walked her to the door.

"Thanks for joining me tonight," I said, running a finger over her erect nipple.

Fuck, she was gorgeous in her blue dress, with that red hair spilling around her shoulders.

I wasn't going to ask to come up. I needed to take my time with this hottie. Try the slow burn for a change.

She just smiled at me and wrapped her arms around my neck, pulling me to her one last time.

"Would you like to come up?" she asked.

Fuck yeah.

But I wasn't going to.

"I'd like nothing more than that, but I think I'll save it for another time. That cool?"

In the dark of her apartment building doorway, I watched disappointment wash over her face.

Which made me happy.

"You'll give me a raincheck, won't you? I've got plans for you, baby, and they involve your being naked."

And my dick being hard. Really hard.

That got her to smile. "Oooh. I likey. Until then."

She pressed a code to get into her building, and I walked back to my cab.

I'd been seconds from heading up to her apartment, and now I was going home with blue balls.

But she'd be worth the wait. No doubt about it.

CHAPTER ELEVEN

Cricket

Well, damn.

I sadly stepped out of my evening gown, hanging it in the back of my closet where it would probably say forever, and recapped the night.

I invite a guy up to my apartment, and he turns me down. Icing on the cake for one of the most memorable evenings of my life.

Well, it wasn't all bad. I liked Halliday. She rocked.

But those old biddies trashing me in the ladies' room. Fuck me. Where did they get off? They're lucky I didn't take off my earrings and show them how girls from Rhode Island take care of business.

Of course, it would have been unseemly to put up my dukes, so I'd resorted to an equally sordid but more genteel manner of expressing my displeasure.

And in the end, I probably hurt the bitch right where she lived, on her expensive designer evening dress, which she had to wear the rest of the night with people politely looking away in embarrassment for her.

"Spill your wine, Mrs. Cazzo? Have you tried soda water? It works wonders."

I could imagine the steam rising from her ears.

And it felt damn good.

I'd surprised myself with my superb acting job, pretending someone had bumped into me in order to spill all over that bitch's dress. Even Talbot had been convinced. I'd have to remember that one. A real Washington, D.C. middle finger.

Yeah, I was figuring this town out.

Next, I'd try it on that creep at work, Sadie.

Chalk it up to being a—what had they called me? A rube?

What the hell was a rube, anyway? Couldn't they do better than that? Personally, I was really taken by Halliday's term—cunty bitch. That had some serious teeth to it.

And because Talbot had so unkindly turned down my invitation for some nookie, after I'd hung up my fabulous second-hand dress, I crawled between the covers and reached into my nightstand for Brad Pitt.

Yeah, I had a nickname for my vibrator.

Actually, I had two vibes. The other one was called George Clooney. I mean, did it get much better than those two guys? Actually, I wouldn't mind an Idris Elba, but does a girl really need three vibrators?

I thought back to how Talbot had run his fingers under my ass and how he hungrily looked at my cleavage, half-spilling out of the top of my dress.

Which had been by design, of course.

But most magical was how he looked me in the eye at the ball. Like there was no one else in the room. I hadn't expected that.

I might be forced to forget about getting an interview with the guy, but it looked like I could end up with something way better.

"Wayne, I think we're caught up on the preorders." That's what I liked to call the obits we wrote in advance.

It bugged him that I called them that, but I didn't really care. I was doing all the work so figured I could have a snappy nickname if I wanted. I'd earned it. But Wayne wasn't about having fun at work.

I mean, a person who goes to funerals for kicks was not going to be the life of the office party.

He looked up from the desk in his tidy cube. No one dumped their dead office equipment there.

"Oh, that's great, Cricket. Guess we can slow down a bit since we're ahead of the game. Unless a plane full of a sports team goes down in the Andes or something."

He dropped his head back and cackled, like a character from *The Addams Family*.

I left him laughing at his joke and wandered back to my desk to soothe myself with a puppy video or two.

Shit. In the distance, I heard Ken, our editor in chief, making the rounds. He occasionally did that, regaling the staff with stories about his encounters with the Washington heavy hitters he considered close, personal friends.

My cube was not usually on his socializing route, but given that he was expecting a story from me, I figured I was next in line. I peered over the cube wall, and while he had his back turned to me, I grabbed my bag and slipped out of the office.

I had a plan.

I took the Metro to Capitol Hill and made my way into the pressroom using my work credentials. If I couldn't deliver a story on Talbot, I'd try to find a story on something else. I had Ken's ear, so to speak, and didn't want to lose my chance.

The chance I'd been waiting for, for a *long* time. The chance that would prove to myself and everyone else that yes, I did indeed belong in Washington, D.C., and in particular, at one of the country's top newspapers.

I needed this. I was tired of that nagging thought in the back of my head that my ambitions were beyond my abilities.

Once in the press room, I scanned for a familiar face.

"Cricket, hi. What are you doing here?"

I looked into the kind eyes of our political reporter, Ed. He'd always been so nice, I could hardly believe he covered politics. Seemed like a job for some backslapping, smarmy suck up. Not unlike our editor in chief.

I lowered my voice and looked around the room. Reporters were the nosiest people on Earth, and I needed to keep my failings private. "Well, remember how Ken wanted me to do that story on Talbot Richardson?"

"Yeah. Any luck with that? His press secretary shut me down flat."

I walked him over to a quiet corner.

"Well, I've kind of been hanging out with him," I said.

He nodded. "You guys are friends from college, right?"

Ugh. That shit was going to follow me around forever.

I skated past the question, including the fact that Talbot and I had had a major make out session in the back of a cab. "So, you know how until the paternity suit is resolved, he's flat-out not giving interviews? Problem is, this is my big chance to write some real news for the paper. I don't know if Ken will give me another."

He thought for a moment and smiled, walking me away from the crowd. "I might have something for you."

Holy crap. I wanted to throw my arms around the man. Maybe even give him my first-born child.

"Really, Ed? That would be so awesome. I was hoping I could pick up something. Anything. Big or small, I don't care. I just need to show him I can investigate and write something other than obits."

"Okay. Here's the scoop. It's not anything huge, but it could be a good start. Senator Cazzo has a bill that bans puppy mills. I know you do that dog walking volunteer stuff, so this is right up your alley."

Tears sprang to my eyes.

"The paper hasn't covered this, but it might garner a lot of interest. The public is pretty outraged over the whole issue." He patted me on the shoulder.

"Ed, I don't know how I can ever thank you. I'm gonna start on this right now."

He laughed. "Christ, someone's gotta give you a break. It's how we all get started."

He wandered away to gab with some of his reporter friends from the New York Times, and I started frantically researching the puppy mill issue on my phone. Just as I was digging in, I got a text from Bridget.

how was the ball? did you feel like cinderella? LOL
it was okay. I'll fill you in via phone
and the guy?
so hot. OMG
any zesty sessions?
eh. a little
shit. the twins are screaming. see ya

My text chat with Bridget reminded me of our upcoming trip to Block Island, and my recent tetanus shot courtesy of her adorable husband. The plan was for Simon's parents to be over from the U.K. to watch their three kids. But to be honest, I wouldn't have minded them coming with. I loved those little rugrats.

Besides, it wasn't like I'd be bringing a plus-one, anyway. The douchebag surgeon was enough to turn me off dating for the rest of my life.

But, there *was* Talbot.

Nah. I couldn't invite him. We didn't have that kind of relationship.

Ed turned to me from the group where he stood, threw me a thumbs up, and headed out.

Now, if *I* could only believe in myself the way *he* did.

Puppy mills were the enemy of any animal lover and a particularly big insult for a fanatic like me. The mills treated their dogs like livestock—the females were kept constantly pregnant, and the puppies were poorly cared for and often arrived at their first homes unvaccinated, with fleas, kennel cough, malnourishment, and worse.

And when the female dogs could no longer produce litters? They were put down.

It was all about money and nothing about having compassion for another living being.

I know I was supposed to be objective about this in order to report both sides accurately, but in this instance, I didn't care.

And it seemed there was someone, a Senator Cazzo

from Michigan, who felt as passionately about this as I did. I was going to get his perspective and help the Washington Chronicle shed light on this important issue. And maybe help my career along a little bit, in the process.

Funny name, Cazzo. I could swear I'd heard it somewhere before. His online picture looked familiar, too.

I headed in the direction of the Senate building toward Senator Cazzo's office. I was pretty sure he wouldn't speak with me, which would be consistent with my overall but limited experience trying to interview senators. But, there was a chance his press secretary might be able to share some insights.

As I approached the office, an elegantly dressed older couple was exiting his office door. I glanced back at the senator's bio on my phone.

Holy crap. It was him.

"Senator Cazzo!" I called.

He slowly turned, as did his companion, and frowned when he realized he didn't recognize me.

I extended my hand. "I'm Cricket Curtain from the Washington Chronicle. Do you have a moment for a couple questions about your puppy mill legislation?

He looked at his companion and forced a smile. "Sure, I have a couple minutes. What can I help you with?"

My heart leapt. Was this my big chance?

While I flipped my notebook open, I glanced at the woman next to him.

Oh, shit.

Now I knew where I'd heard the name Cazzo.

The woman at the ball, who I'd spilled the wine on? None other than Senator Cazzo's wife.

Oops.

But I was nothing if not a fast thinker.

"Hello, ma'am, I hope you don't mind my taking a moment of the senator's time here."

She opened her mouth to answer me, but I cut her off. "You know, I saw a woman who looked like you at a ball the other night. But she was much older than you. And her evening dress was stained with red wine. Imagine that."

As she narrowed her eyes at me, I turned to her husband. "Senator, I'm glad to see your commitment to outlawing puppy mills. How did you get interested in this?"

"The Humane Society in my state approached me with this. They made their case and when they did, it was a no-brainer. Puppy mills need to go."

"How long do you think it will take the legislation to pass?" I asked.

He pursed his lips. "I hope this year. You know how slowly legislation works its way through Congress."

I smiled politely, even though I had no idea how long it took for a bill to become a law.

"How will you make sure legitimate breeders don't get caught up in this, and that their businesses remain safe?"

"I propose that all breeders go through some sort of certification program with regular inspections."

Sounded great to me. A little rehearsed, but that was okay.

"Thank you for your time, Senator. You two have a lovely day now."

The senator shook my hand, and I smiled brightly at his wife, who returned a sour stare. The thrill of victory pulsed through me as I realized I'd gotten some decent info for an article, and I'd managed to get under the skin of a nasty bitch.

I stepped to the side of the hallway to finish my notes, and Senator and Mrs. Cazzo continued on their way, speaking a little louder in the echo-y hallway than they realized.

He patted his wife on the back. "Sweetie, you didn't look old last night. Don't worry."

"Oh, shut up, Frank."

As if my encounter with Senator and Mrs. Cazzo hadn't been weird enough, the next text message to arrive on my phone certainly was.

I looked up from typing up notes from my chat with Cazzo, when a text from Talbot buzzed my phone. My heart slammed against my chest as I thought back to the way he'd kissed me in that cab.

If the driver hadn't insisted on ending our make out session, who knew how far it would have gone.

Which reminded, me. I needed to remember to pick up batteries for Brad Pitt.

Or was it George Clooney?

My phone buzzed with a text from none other than Talbot.

busy this weekend?

i might be . who's asking?

come to new york with me. for the weekend.

what???

Wait. Had he meant to send that text to *me*? No. No way.

What. The. Fuck.

Before I could talk myself into even considering such an invitation, the phone rang.

"Are you serious?" I didn't even say hello.

I also looked over the cube wall to make sure Wayne wasn't around.

"Hello to you too, Miss Curtain. And yes, I am. We'll fly in my dad's jet and stay at my Soho condo."

Dad's jet?

Soho condo?

Was this a trick?

Slow down, cowgirl. As curious as I was about his offer, I wasn't interested in being some senator's fuck of the week.

Or fuck of the weekend.

Even though he'd kissed me very nicely. And was a volunteer at the community center. And hadn't called me out about spilling my wine on that old biddy, Mrs. Cazzo.

My resolve, if I ever had any to begin with, was failing.

"Your dad has a plane?" It was all I could think to say.

I couldn't go away with him for a weekend... *could I?*

"He does, and it's available for us to use, which doesn't happen too often. We'll go to a nice dinner, walk the High Line. Whatever you feel like."

Oh, my god. All those times I'd followed him around campus, and now, he wanted to spend a weekend with me?

"Um, I need to check one thing. Can I get right back to you?"

Smooth, very smooth.

"Sure. I'm running, too. Chief of staff is here. Hey, Bruce—"

And he was gone.

I was stunned. Like so stunned I couldn't even watch a puppy video. This was serious shit.

Ohmygod. What would I wear?

I called Bridget.

"Hi sweetie, I was just thinking of you today," she said.

"Ohmygod, you will not believe this. Do you have a sec?"

"Yeah. I have five minutes left on my break. What's up? *Oh, hi honey*. That's funny, Simon just walked by."

I pictured the two of them in their scrubs, the Ken and Barbie of the hospital world. *That's* how good-looking they were.

"Remember the senator guy? He asked me to go away with him for the weekend."

She gasped so loudly I had to look over my shoulder to make sure no one had heard.

"No. Fucking. Way."

"What do I do? I don't know what to do," I whispered.

"What? Go with him, for heaven's sake. Are you kidding?"

I could see her rolling her eyes.

"Yeah. I mean, I probably will."

Various hospital beeps sounded in the background. "Oh, damn. My break's up. But go get some nice underwear, and for heaven's sake, get waxed down there."

Click.

I waited a full eight hours before I texted Talbot that, yes, I'd join him for the weekend.

I'd already bought the new lingerie and been to the waxer's.

CHAPTER TWELVE

Talbot

I t was a great day for a quick flight up to New York, and I was psyched for a break from D.C.

"Does your dad really have a plane?" Cricket asked, looking out the cab window at the private airfield alongside Dulles International Airport.

I looked at her next to me. She was so goddamn cute with her skinny jeans, plain white blouse, and the bandana around her neck. "Yup. You'll enjoy it. I promise."

My parents were going to love her. I hoped.

"I'm so excited." She grabbed my hand and squeezed it just before we hopped out of the cab at the airplane hangar. She slung a backpack over her shoulder, and I grabbed both our wheelie suitcases.

God, I loved a woman who didn't over pack.

We were heading for the hangar's office when the flight concierge approached us with a clipboard in hand. "Senator Richardson, good to see you. Your father's plane is ready to go. Let me take you to it."

"Hey, Tom. You can still call me Talbot, you know."

He laughed. "Sounds good."

I was used to private planes—I'd been flying on them for as long as I could remember—but Cricket wasn't. It was refreshing to see her excitement instead of the boredom of the women I usually ended up with, who yawned at everything.

I hadn't been sure, when I'd extended the invitation, whether Cricket would spend the weekend with me. But I was persistent. I suspected her reticence was a matter of principle and not practice. I mean, hell, she *had* invited me up to her apartment after the ball.

But to spend a weekend together? That was a different story. She was *wary* of me.

And I could not blame her.

Christ, I'd been accused of being someone's baby daddy, and it was front page news everywhere. Yeah, my attorney was handling the work of proving me innocent, but the longer it took, the more the chattering classes whispered and made assumptions.

And, even when I *was* exonerated, which I *would* be, people would still look at me with a suspicious eye for a long time to come. It was just a fact.

I also got why someone might hesitate to go out with a senator. Status-seeking gold diggers were all over us, but the self-possessed women, the kind you might take home to your parents, were careful shoppers, so to speak.

Which made them all the more desirable.

So, in the end, it had taken some convincing over several text messages before Cricket accepted my invitation. I'd even offered her my guest room. No assumptions would be made.

And now, she was darting around the inside of my father's jet, like a kid in a candy store, exploring every nook and cranny, and driving me crazy wishing I could lower her tight jeans all the way down to her ankles.

"Oh, my god, this is beautiful," she gushed over the dark leather chairs and big, porthole windows.

I followed her gaze, but what I really wanted to do was follow her curvy ass.

"It's so much bigger than I thought it would be. Are we the only ones here?"

I stowed our bags in a closet and grabbed champagne from the fridge.

"We are. Except for the pilot. A longer flight would have more crew, but for D.C. to New York, we're all set."

I popped open the bubbly, and we clinked glasses.

"Thank you, Talbot. This is such a treat."

It sure was.

"Thank you for joining me. It's going to be fun."

She leaned forward to kiss me, just as the pilot barged in to say hi.

"Oh. Excuse me." He waited for us to compose ourselves.

"Welcome aboard, Senator. Welcome, Ms. Curtain. This will be a quick jump up to the airport in Teterboro, where I believe a car will take you into Manhattan. Enjoy your flight."

With that, he disappeared into the cockpit.

She lowered her voice. "It's so weird, not having to go through security and all."

I laughed. "You don't have to whisper. We're not going to get in trouble."

She leaned back in her seat, just opposite mine, and placed a bare foot on my knee.

Was this the ankle that she sprained? Or was it the other?

I decided to let it go.

"You dropped your sneaker." I gestured to her the white Converse on the floor.

She smiled defiantly. This was going to be a very good weekend.

Since she was offering me her foot, I set down my drink to massage her arch. She sighed, closed her eyes, and leaned her head back on her chair.

"Oh, my god, that's heavenly," she purred.

I took the opportunity to run a finger up the center of her foot, tickling her until she screamed.

"Give me my foot back!" She tried to wrestle it out of my hand, but I had her by the ankle.

"I don't think so," I said, stroking the bottom of her foot and sending her into squirming hysterics again.

"What'll you give me to stop? You know, life is all about negotiations," I said.

She slammed her hands on her armrest. "Anything. Just stop tickling me."

"All right, then." I stopped torturing the bottom on her foot but kept my grip on her ankle. "Open your blouse."

Her eyes widened. "What? Here? Are you kidding? What if the pilot walks out?"

Seriously?

"The pilot is *flying the plane*."

She craned her neck to see behind me. "Oh. Right."

I ran a fingernail under the soft part of her arch.

"Okay!" she screamed.

Her fingers began to unbutton her shirt, opening it just enough so I could see the lace on her bra.

"There. Now may I have my leg back?"

I rolled my eyes. "Okay, your blouse is unbuttoned. But it's not open. I can't see anything."

"Oh, *that's* what you meant. Okay."

She unbuttoned her blouse further, revealing more of what looked like a very sexy bra.

"Keep going," I demanded.

With a deep breath, she opened another button.

And my dick was standing at full attention.

"That's not enough."

"How's this?" she asked with an impatient sigh. She

pulled her blouse the rest of the way open and halfway down her shoulders.

What a sight she was, staring at me with delicious defiance, her blouse hanging off, with a flimsy little bra holding her big, round tits.

"Touch yourself now."

She sighed deeply, and when she realized I wasn't backing off, acquiesced by running her hands over her breasts, stopping to pull her nipples through the bra fabric.

"Pull them out."

At this point, I'd released her foot and rearranged the erection in my pants, which was on the verge of becoming painful.

And just as I'd asked, her milky tits popped out of her bra, nipples hard from pulling. And what fucking awesome tits they were.

Before she realized it, I was on my knees in front of her, pushing her breasts together and running my lips over them to taste their sweetness.

"Fuck, baby, your tits are great," I murmured.

"I want something now," she said.

My head popped up. "What's that?"

"Well, I can see you have an erection. I want to see it."

Holy fuck. A woman after my own heart.

I moved back into my chair. "Keep playing with your tits," I demanded.

Unzipping my fly, I fished through the opening in

my boxers and pulled out my raging hard-on. I stroked it slowly.

"If I do this too long, I might come, baby."

She licked her lips. "I'd like to see that."

I took a deep breath and put my dick back in my pants and zipped myself up. "I bet you would."

She rolled her eyes and put herself back together just as the pilot announced we were getting ready to land.

Cricket stared out of the car taking us to my apartment and craned her neck to see the skyscrapers.

"Last time I was here, I was with a bunch of girl-friends, and we stayed at some horrible hotel." She laughed. "We had a blast."

I pulled her to me, my cock still semi-hard. "Well, I hope I can show you as good a time this weekend."

"You better."

It felt good to be back in the city. I never liked being away from New York for too long, and god knew I missed my apartment.

When we arrived, I opened my front door so Cricket could enter first. I'd let the cleaning lady know I was returning, and she'd taken the time to air out the place and put fresh sheets on the beds.

Cricket did a three-sixty to take in the living room. "This place is insane."

I loved it, too. "The building used to be an elevator factory. It sat empty for many years until some investors renovated it."

"So cool."

"Go ahead. Look around."

I followed her, wanting to reacquaint myself as well. I hadn't realized how much I missed it, as well as the smells and noise of New York. They weren't always pleasant, but like anything truly familiar, they were comforting.

She ran up the stairs to the loft bedroom, and I gave her a moment to snoop. Women loved bedrooms, as if they were a window into your soul. I never quite got it, their tendency to gather information like honeybees on the hunt, but it was all good.

Evolution, I supposed.

Back when I'd gotten my place, my mother had hounded me to let her decorate it. Fearing she'd outfit every surface in flowery pastel chintz, I resisted for a long time, with only a bed to sleep on and a sofa for watching TV. It was all a guy needed, really. But when she convinced me she'd make the place understated and masculine, I caved.

And I was damn glad I did. She'd delivered a modern set-up with muted grays and had limited herself to placing one houseplant in a corner, which somehow still thriving despite my neglect.

When I reached the top step of my loft, I found Cricket sitting on the edge of my bed like a happy little kid. All I could do was lean in the doorway and watch. If I got any closer, we'd be in all night and miss our dinner reservation.

Although, that wouldn't be so bad. And it actually looked like that might just happen.

Once she had me as her audience, my red-haired vixen unbuttoned her blouse just enough to once again show off the top of her lacy bra. If I could have taken a photo, I would have. Sultry but sweet.

After tormenting me for a moment, she one-by-one opened all her buttons, tossing the blouse to the floor. She'd already kicked off her sneakers, so she stood and shimmied her jeans down her curvy hips, leaving her standing in a white lace thong that matched her bra.

It was sheer.

And she was shaved.

Fuck me.

She pouted. "What? You don't like?" She ran her hands across her stomach and up to her tits, which she kneaded and pushed together.

Alrighty then.

"Oh, I like." I nodded slowly but remained in the doorway, fighting the urge to pull out my cock and give it the stroking it was begging for.

"You wanna come over?" she asked, beckoning me with her finger.

"Not yet. First, I want to see you touch yourself. Down there." I lowered my gaze to where the white lace barely covered her.

A slight blush washed over her face, but she held her head up in defiance. After a moment's hesitation, her hand slipped into her panties.

Beautiful.

"Good girl. Keep going."

Her gaze remained glued to mine as her chest rose and fell. Unable to stand it any longer, I pulled out my hard-on and moved my hand from root to tip as I watched her slide her own hand in and out of her panties.

"Taste yourself."

Her gaze burning, she drew two fingers to her mouth. Closing her eyes, she sucked.

Enough torture.

I strode to where she sat at the end of my bed and lifted her completely onto the mattress, pinning her hands above her head. I could smell her arousal, and when I pressed my mouth to hers, I tasted it on her lips.

She arched, grinding her heated skin against my hard cock and as I moved my lips down her neck, her breathing grew ragged.

Just how I liked it.

I whipped off my own clothes and tossed them to the floor. Reaching for her panties, I hooked a finger in each side and slowly shimmied the lace off her hips. I ran my lips across the light sprinkle of freckles across her stomach and worked my way down.

When I reached her pussy, I opened her with my

tongue, running up and down her slit from ass to clit. She was soaked with excitement as I'd suspected she'd be, and when I entered her with a finger and then two, she arched and moaned.

Damn. I knew this woman was hot, but the way she was responding was beyond anything I'd imagined while jerking off.

Yep, I'd jerked off thinking about her.

With one hand on my cock, I zeroed in on her hard clit, loving the moans filling my room.

"Talbot, I'm gonna come, oh my god," she murmured.

That was my signal to start pumping her pussy and just as I did, she began to convulse in the hottest fucking way I'd ever seen. She grabbed my hair and pushed my face down as she creamed on me and the sheets beneath us.

While she was still coming down, I scooted up on her chest, putting my dick between her tits.

"Yes," she whispered, moving my hands aside and pushing her tits together for me.

I was so goddamn close that with three or four thrusts, I exploded over her chest, neck and chin.

I lay down, wrapped my arms around her, and forgot all about the dinner reservation.

CHAPTER THIRTEEN

CRICKET

"Cricket, wake up. I'm starving," Talbot said, shaking me.

I opened my eyes to his running a warm cloth over my chest to clean up the cum I was covered in.

"Wow. We fell asleep." I looked around his awesome apartment. So different from what you'd see in D.C. "Thank you. I guess I could also just take a shower."

He sat back on the bed. "Yeah. Why don't you do that, and I'll order Chinese delivery? We can watch a movie. We missed our dinner reservation."

"Are you complaining?" I teased.

"What do you think?"

He dug into a closet and pulled on sweats that hung loosely on his hips, showing off a thin line of hair that disappeared beneath the drawstring waistband.

Holy shit. I was ready for the next round. To hell with the Chinese food. I might starve, but I'd die happy.

He handed me his bathrobe and got on the phone to order.

His loft-condo thing—I wasn't really sure what to call it—was freaking amazing. Big, open spaces with polished concrete floors, decorated in soft grays and whites. He'd told me his mom had decorated it for him, and I was completely impressed with the woman's taste. It was deliciously masculine, but not to the point where it looked like a cliché bachelor pad.

And his bathroom, good lord. There was an enormous stall with three shower heads and a built-in seat in the corner in case you wanted to just sit and enjoy the perfect water pressure.

I was tempted, but knowing he was out there waiting for me lit a fire under my ass. I cleaned up and washed my hair, and when I stepped out of the shower, I realized the bathroom floor was heated.

Was there anything this guy didn't have?

"There's a hair dryer under the sink," he hollered from downstairs.

I got myself as presentable as necessary and descended the loft to the living room, where he'd spread out ten or so Chinese food containers on a giant coffee table. He was flicking through the cable channels and settled on *Casablanca*.

Perfection. I was in love.

Cripes. No, I was not in love.

"Ever seen this movie?" he asked, handing me a glass of wine.

I took a sip. Of course, it was the best zinfandel I'd ever tasted.

"Not in a long time. Perfect movie for a night in with takeout."

I sank into the sofa and after a few bites, Talbot pulled me to him and we settled into the sad story of the ill-fated lovers, Rick and Ilsa. I couldn't remember the last time I'd felt so comfortable, safe, and warm. Maybe I never had. There I was, snuggling with a delicious hunk of a man in his Manhattan apartment, with an abundance of takeout cartons to choose from, watching a classic movie in black and white.

I wanted to pinch myself to make sure I wasn't dreaming.

By the end of the movie, when Rick and Ilsa part on the airfield, I had tears streaming down my cheeks. Talbot didn't make a big deal over my blubbering, simply dabbing my face with a napkin. He kissed me on the head and pressed the remote.

I, unfortunately, responded with a huge yawn.

"You know what? I'm tired, too."

We put away our dinner mess and made our way to the loft.

I stopped at the top of the stairs. "Wait. Wasn't I supposed to take the guest room?"

I couldn't resist. Sometimes, I was bratty that way.

He frowned for a millisecond, then smiled. "Yes, right. I almost forgot. Follow me."

We went back downstairs and at the other end of the condo, he showed me to a guest room.

"I think you'll be comfortable here. You have your own bathroom, and I can see the housekeeper put out fresh towels for you."

He was playing my game. Good for him, what a sport.

Now let's see who would cave first.

"Goodnight," I said with a chaste kiss.

"Holler if you need anything," he said from the doorway.

As I watched him turn to leave, I plopped down on the edge of the bed. I thought for sure he'd come back and insist I join him.

I looked around the room and grabbed a National Geographic from the nightstand. As I flipped through an article on the Galapagos, I started to doze off, only to be wakened by dropping the magazine in my face.

Well. He'd never come back to get me.

He was calling my bluff. Fine. He could be the winner if he wanted.

Tiptoeing, I crossed the floor and silently made my way upstairs. I slipped off my robe and climbed into bed next to him.

"Took you long enough," he said, pulling me into his arms.

"So, what's on the agenda today?" I asked when I was dressed and ready to go. "Shall we take a long walk? See a bit of the city?"

He buttoned up his white linen shirt and checked his watch. "My parents just called. They're coming into the city to meet us for brunch."

Um, what?

Had he just said I was to meet his parents? Because that's what it had sounded like.

I collapsed on the end of the bed, my legs too wobbly at the news to hold me up. "Um, come again?"

Running his fingers through his thick black hair, he smiled at me. "My parents. We're having brunch with them."

I couldn't even string two words together. I just stared.

He must have spotted the confusion on my face because he sat next to me on the bed, and took one of my hands in both of his. "They're really nice. It's no big deal. Just a spur of the moment thing. It'll be fun. They were coming into the city to play Bridge with friends."

Clearly there was no backing out. So, I took a deep breath and forced myself to be a big girl. "Okay. Let's go." I hoped he wouldn't call me out on my forced cheer.

When we arrived at his dad's club, Talbot's parents were already at the table. I grinned broadly, like I met handsome senator's parents at fancy clubs all the time. His father smiled, but his mom's steely gaze pierced through me, leaving me with cold goose bumps.

How did I know that look? I'd seen it that night at the ball. Talbot's mom was just the kind of woman who'd trash talk someone in the ladies' room and then smile in their face.

And I had to sit right next to her. And I wouldn't be spilling anything down the front of her dress.

The warm contentment of the night before faded into oblivion as my stomach tied itself into knots, and hand shaking as I picked up my coffee cup.

Talbot's dad passed me a platter of buttermilk biscuits. I loved those suckers. My stress was going to unravel itself really quickly because these babies were the perfect antidote for meet-the-parents anxiety.

"Last time I saw my son was in D.C. a couple weeks ago. He tried to kill me with Indian food." He laughed, and Mrs. Richardson gazed at him like he'd said something brilliant.

"C'mon, Dad. You enjoyed it. You told me so."

Mr. Richardson nodded. "I did. You proved to me that I actually like Indian food."

I decided to join the conversation. "So, will you be having it again?"

But before he could respond, Mrs. Richardson did for him. "Oh, no. That was a one-time thing. We don't eat that sort of food. Those *ethnic* restaurants are so dirty," she said, wrinkling her nose in disgust. "If *I'd* been there, we'd never have gone."

Guess Ethiopian was out of the question, then.

"So, Cricket, how'd you end up with such a name?" Mr. Richardson asked.

"My given name is actually Christine. But when I was a baby, a neighborhood kid couldn't pronounce it, and called me Cricket. It stuck."

Talbot's dad nodded politely, and his mom just looked at me.

Guess they didn't find the story as charming as some people did.

Mrs. Richardson took a deep breath. "So, what do you do with your days, Cricket?

"I work at the Washington Chronicle, and I am a volunteer at the puppy rescue agency called DogHouse. Say, did you know Talbot and I went to college together...?"

I babbled on until our brunch was served. I could see my audience was only marginally interested, but out of nervousness, I couldn't stop.

When my food was delivered, Mrs. Richardson looked at my plate like there was a dead rat on it.

I looked at my breakfast special, too, because I was starving, having chattered away all my anxiety. I dove into my French toast, fried eggs, bacon, and sausage. Oh, and a fruit bowl, as well.

I'd been dying for a Bloody Mary, but no one else had ordered alcohol.

Mrs. Richardson gently cracked the shell of her hard-boiled egg.

I wasn't sure if she was looking at my breakfast with envy or disgust.

Or maybe she was still hungry after her one egg?

Talbot's dad moved his head closer to his son's and was speaking in hushed tones. I could make out only a few words, but it had to be about the paternity suit.

I seriously didn't understand why they couldn't just put that issue to bed. But there must have been more to it than I knew.

Which was fine. I didn't need the nitty gritty details.

Mrs. Richardson seemed to realize she was stuck talking with me while her son and husband huddled.

"So, how did you and Talbot meet?" Her expression could not have indicated any less interest.

"I was jogging on the towpath in Georgetown and twisted my ankle. He came along and helped me to my car. We ran into each other a couple times after that and went for coffee."

"Well, isn't that charming."

She reached for her teacup with both hands and pulled it to her lips for the world's daintiest sip.

Was she for real?

Just to make her head explode, I dipped my biscuit into the egg on my plate and stuffed a giant bite into my mouth.

That should shut her up.

And it did. She turned her nose like she'd smelled

something decaying. She looked at her watch and reached across the table to tap her husband's arm.

"Darling, we need to head out for our Bridge game."

"Oh!" he said. "You're right."

He took a big swig of his coffee and stood, pulling Mrs. Richardson's chair out for her.

Talbot hopped to his feet too.

Shit. Was I supposed to stand?

But before I could, Mrs. Richardson extended her hand. "Cricket, it was lovely."

Before I could answer, she turned to her son. "So good to see you, honey. Call me later, okay?"

"Thank you for joining us, Cricket. Good luck at the paper," Mr. Richardson said.

"Good luck at Bridge," I called after them, but they'd already hustled outside, where they jumped into a cab hailed by the doorman.

I could finally breathe and did so with a loud exhale.

"Well, that was fun," Talbot said.

Then he noticed the expression on my face.

"What?" he asked.

I didn't want to make a big deal, but his mom had suggested they chat later, and I had a feeling I might be the subject of the conversation.

"Your mom wasn't exactly warm."

He scratched his head. "Yeah, she's like that. But don't worry about it. I don't pay her any attention. Hey, what do you say we go check out the High Line?"

Way to change the subject.

He stood and pulled my chair out.

"Oh, yeah. Let's go. Hey, what about the check?" I asked.

"It gets charged to my father's account."

He took my arm, and we headed for the door.

The relaxed feeling I'd had the night before?

Gone. Completely gone.

And I still didn't know how I was going to get my interview.

The flight back to D.C. was as quick as the flight up, and when our cab pulled up in front of my apartment, Talbot got out with me and pulled my things out of the trunk.

"Thank you for a great weekend." I grabbed my backpack and wheelie bag.

"Sure you don't want me to carry these in for you?" he offered.

Couldn't blame him for trying.

"Oh, I've got them. I'm super tired. Gonna hit the sack and get to work early tomorrow." I was nearly done with my puppy mill story and was counting on springing it on Ken. I was sure he'd ask about my Talbot story, and I was hoping this would appease him.

Besides, I didn't want Talbot to know that our brunch with his parents was eating at me.

"Okay, then. Talk to you tomorrow." He kissed my cheek and got back in the cab.

The second I got into my apartment, I called Bridget.

"Oh, my god. How was it?" she asked.

The sounds of gurgling babies filled the background.

"Oh, boy. It started off great. Sexy, romantic. I was in heaven. Then, I met his parents."

She gasped. "Oh, shit. I take it from your tone it was not the most pleasant. You know how Simon's parents were to me when we first met. It was horrible. I was the gold-digging sad-sack single mother with baggage to spare. But they came around and now I can't imagine life without them. 'Course having the twins kind of cemented the relationship."

"I get that. But these people—I mean, I don't live in their world. I don't belong there. And his parents—well, they were less than thrilled with me. At least, his mom seemed that way. She was so snobbish, all looking down on me and stuff."

I sank into my sofa and tried to swallow away the lump that was growing in my throat.

Same old, same old.

Always on the outside looking in.

The world was some people's oyster. Mine? Not so much.

Bridget sighed. "I'm sorry, girl. They should be thrilled you were spending time with their son. Fucking people. I hate that they didn't properly appreciate you, and I hate that they made you feel badly. Did you bring it up with Talbot?"

"Kind of. I didn't want to dwell on it. It's not like he could do much about it and I didn't want to ruin the weekend with whining."

"Well, you don't need that crap. Move on. There are nice men out there. Just look at Simon."

Sure. Simon was one in a million. Everyone knew that. Yet Bridget made it sound like there were clones of him all over the place, ripe for the picking.

Well, there weren't.

Fact.

"Cricket! Hey!" someone shouted after me.

I turned to see who it was.

Shit.

It was the surgeon guy, Harry. From Match.com. The one who'd asked for separate checks.

A real prince, that one.

He came running across the street like we were old friends. "Hi there. I left you a couple messages after you left me in that bar."

Oh, for heaven's sake. Doesn't everyone know that if someone ditches you, or doesn't return your calls, it's because they don't want to?

I didn't want to be mean, but *move on, buddy*.

"Oh, right," I lied as if I'd totally forgotten. "Sorry 'bout that."

He was in his scrubs, of course with his Georgetown University Hospital ID prominently displayed. "Hey, my work is having a paint ball get together this weekend. I can bring someone. Would you like to join me?" he asked. "It's fifty dollars a person. I can get you a ticket and you can pay me back later."

Oh, for fuck's sake. Was he serious?

"Thanks, Harry. But I don't think I'm interested."

Why did I say I didn't *think* I was interested? I *knew* I wasn't interested.

"Are you sure? It sounds really fun. I thought you'd enjoy it since you don't have much going on."

What the fucking fuck?

"I gotta go, Harry. I'm late for my volunteering gig." I took off down the sidewalk, trotting as fast as my platform sandals would let me. I had to get away from that creep before he slimed me any more than he already had.

"Okay, see ya, Cricket," he called after me. "Let me know if you change your mind. You still have my number, right?"

I dashed inside DogHouse and leaned against the wall to catch my breath. The volunteer coordinator caught sight of me and brought me to my first assignment of the evening, to bottle feed a tiny pup whose mother had died.

I cradled the little guy, whose eyes were not even

open yet. He was completely vulnerable, and it was so unfair life had started out so hard for him. I took him to a chair in the corner where I could be alone with him, and I let my tears flow. He didn't even notice as they fell on his head. He just wanted his formula, and he noisily slurped away.

When I left two hours later, I just happened to walk by the community center, and just happened to walk in to see what was going on in the basketball auditorium. The usual gaggle of pre-teen boys was awkwardly practicing, losing the ball, missing baskets, and making enough noise to fill a stadium.

And their coach? Well, it wasn't Talbot.

I should have known. Once he got busy, he had no time for volunteering. He probably didn't even say goodbye to the kids before he bailed on them.

Sometimes it was best to just cut your losses. Although it seemed like someone had just cut mine for me.

CHAPTER FOURTEEN

TALBOT

It was a good thing I'd gotten away for the weekend with Cricket because it sure as hell looked like I wouldn't be seeing the light of day again anytime soon. Congress was in full swing, which meant that I was running like a fucking maniac from one committee meeting to another. I was spending my days dickering with other senators over things like how much funding our highways would get and what should be done about global warming. And then there were my voters who were pissed about the baby daddy fiasco.

The worst of it? I didn't have a spare moment to call Cricket.

And I'd missed several of coaching sessions at the community center. That really killed me. Those kids counted on me.

But I counted on them more.

"Dude, I can barely keep up with you," Bruce said, hustling alongside me.

I was getting a little breathless myself, but since I barely had time for running anymore, this would have to do as my exercise. Unfortunately, I was also sweating like a pig inside my expensive suit.

"Bruce, as my chief of staff, you gotta cut me some slack on this scheduling. You're gonna kill me."

He threw his hands up. "All right, but there's so much going on around here, who knew it would be so fucking crazy—"

I looked around and lowered my voice. "Hey, can you not talk like we're at a keg party? Clean it up."

There was a tap on my arm. "Excuse me. Are you Senator Richardson? Talbot Richardson?"

Bruce's eyebrows rose as we turned to face a petite blonde with an iPhone in her hand.

"Yes, I am. What can I do for you?" I asked.

Her face brightened. "Well, I'm just so excited to meet the youngest senator ever elected. Can I have a picture taken with you?"

Shit, I was late, but you couldn't say no to requests like this. Way too dickish.

"Of course. Bruce, do you mind?"

He tore his eyes away from the woman's cleavage and grabbed her phone, turning the camera multiple ways to get a good shot. Presumably.

She looked at her phone to check the couple

pictures Bruce had taken. "Oh, thank you so much! My friends and I have been following your career," she gushed.

"What's your name, ma'am?" I asked, extending my hand.

She hesitated for a moment, as if she'd forgotten, but recovered quickly. "Jenny. Jenny Hatch."

"It's very nice to meet you, Mrs. Hatch. Now I have to run to a meeting I'm late for." Bruce and I turned to go.

She grabbed my arm. "I'm not Mrs. I'm a *Miss*."

"Okay, then. We'll see you later. Nice meeting you," I called over my shoulder.

We dashed up the steps to the Capitol, but when we got to the top, Bruce stopped me.

He lowered his voice. "She was all over you. What's with the disinterest?"

I shrugged. "You go ask her out if you like her."

A shit-eating grin spread across his face. "Oh, I get it now. You're hung up on that newspaper girl with the weird name."

I took a deep breath to calm myself. "You know, Bruce, you're really beginning to bug the shit out of me."

He held his hands up like a *stop* sign. "Okay. Excuse me. I didn't realize you were on your period."

I turned and walked into the building without him.

When I finally had a moment to call Cricket, she didn't pick up. She didn't return my text, either. At least, not right away.

That was out of character. She was usually tethered to her cell phone like it was growing out of her hand. Had a bunch of people just died and she was busy with her obits?

The weekend away with her, which now felt light-years away, had been better than I'd expected. She was easy-going, a great conversationalist, and a shitload of fun.

And smoking hot in the sack.

We'd not sealed the deal yet, so to speak, but we'd enjoyed each other immensely. I could tell she wanted to take it slow, and even though she came to me in my bed the first night and every night after, I wanted to follow her lead. For the short term, anyway.

Ever since, each time I got in the shower, I had to jerk off to relieve my blue balls. I wanted her, and I wanted her badly.

She'd done a great job with my parents, coming off as smart, interesting, and accomplished. They hadn't warmed to her much, since she wasn't of 'our world,' but I didn't give a shit about that. If they wanted to limit their life experiences, that was on them.

If they didn't appreciate a kick-ass woman like Cricket, well, it was their fucking loss. My only regret was that she was made to feel uncomfortable. *That* was bullshit.

The women in 'our world,' as my mother liked to call them, were, for the most part, spoiled, boring, and vain. They were hard-core husband hunters whose top priority in life was marrying well. Everything else came second.

Even my good friend Halliday was after a daddy figure, which I gave her no end of shit about.

Cricket was not going to slip through my fingers if there was anything I could do about it. And if my afternoon's Senate vote on the environmental bill wasn't too late, I planned track her down at DogHouse before my coaching session at the community center.

With a little time between my meetings, I thought back to the woman I'd just had a photo taken with. Something about her had been off. Unsettling, even, and I couldn't put my finger on it. On my phone I did a quick Google search of her name, and the only one I found looked nothing like the blonde I'd just met.

And why had she hesitated before she told me her name? I texted Bruce.

remember that woman from outside? can you see if you can find her? maybe she's still out there. get her contact info

sure. on my way

A few minutes later, my phone buzzed with his response.

no sign of her. sorry.

Shit.

Before heading into the community center for coaching, I popped my head into DogHouse. Maybe I'd manage to run into the elusive Cricket.

"May I help you, sir?" a woman asked me from behind a desk.

The place was a riot of dog barking. A few puppies had been let out of their cages and ran around like liberated cockroaches.

"Yes, please. I'm looking for Cricket Curtain."

She looked at a schedule posted on the wall. "Hmmm. Not sure when she'll be in next. Sorry."

"No problem. Thank you."

Well, bummer.

"Mister Senator Man, you're back!" one of the kids hollered. "We started without you."

I rubbed a couple sweaty little heads. "That's awesome, guys. I'm psyched to see you, too. I need to run and change but while I do, keep doing your drills, okay?"

"Hey Mister Senator Man, what happened to your girlfriend?

A titter ran through the group.

"You know, the one with the big—"

He didn't get to finish. One of his teammates elbowed him in the chest.

But that didn't slow them down.

"Did she dump you? Because girls dump guys all the time. That's the problem with them." He shook his head sadly.

I wonder how many times he'd been dumped in his ten-year life.

"Guys, she's just a friend." I held my hands up to try to gain some control.

The littlest guy jumped in front of my face. "My mom says a man and a woman can't just be friends. It never works because men always want sex. You gotta get married and shit or just forget about them—"

He was elbowed in the chest before he could finish. "Don't talk like that here. It's not allowed," one of his friends hissed at him.

"Plus, you don't even know what sex is, shorty."

"Okay, everybody. If I don't see some people running the court in about five seconds flat, this practice will be our last."

Eyes widened and my little men fell into line.

"I'll be back in two minutes," I said to them as I went to change, "and I don't want you to stop until then."

In the locker room, I tried calling Cricket again.

"Hi, there," she said.

I put the phone on speaker while I stripped down to my skivvies. "Hey, stranger. I'm sorry I've been so incommunicado. Work has me running day and night."

"That's okay. I'm just finishing my piece on the puppy mills story. Senator Cazzo was really helpful."

I bet he was.

"Hey, did I tell you, he was with his wife? She was

giving me the stink eye the whole time I was talking to him. Wonder if that wine ever came out of her dress."

I didn't know how my parents could be friends with those people. Well, I actually did know how. They were part of 'their world,' as my mother liked to say.

What a shitty world to live in when you had to be friends with people like that.

I heard a ruckus from the basketball court.

"Hey, I'm at the community center and the kids are getting restless. I'd better go. Are you free for dinner tomorrow night?"

I couldn't get the picture out of my mind of her on my bed, her red hair splayed across the sheets, pushing her hungry pussy into my face...

"It just so happens that I am free, yes."

"Awesome. We'll figure out the details later. Looking forward to it."

The noise from the court was getting louder.

"Gotta run!" I said and tossed my phone in a locker.

I ran out to the court to find that the little guy, who'd said a man and woman couldn't be friends, was on the floor being pummeled by the kid who'd told him he didn't know what sex was.

Christ. This place was supposed to be my respite from work, and these ten-year-olds were acting just like the senators I worked with.

Refereeing little men and grown-ups—not really that different, except I think I liked the kids better.

CHAPTER FIFTEEN

CRICKET

Aimee breathlessly stormed my cubicle, looking stunning as always with her narrow skirt, high heels, and messy bun.

"Cricket, did you see the news on the senator you're trying to do the story on?"

"Who, Talbot? I mean, Senator Richardson?"

"Yeah." She gestured for me to follow her. What was going on?

"Richardson is the one you went to college with, right?" she asked.

I followed her into the break room, where the TV on the wall constantly streamed cable news.

What the hell was going on? Everyone else in the room was gathered around the TV, too.

"There is he with the woman who claims he's her

baby daddy. It's true after all!" Aimee cried.

On the TV was a photo of Talbot standing in front of the U.S. Capitol, wearing his sexy half grin, and with his arm around the shoulders of a petite blonde. A very pretty petite blonde.

The caption read: *Photo proves pregnant accuser really knows Senator Richardson.*

Our IT guy, who was pouring himself a new cup of coffee, shook his head sadly. "Guess he can kiss his Senate career goodbye. What a shame. He was good on the environment."

Our sports writer agreed with him. "Some guys just gotta keep it in their pants. I mean, I'm sure a good-looking guy like him can get all the, um, dates he wants. But you gotta be at least a little careful."

I turned and gave each of them a dirty look. They responded by glancing at each other, then heading back to their desks.

"She's pretty, isn't she?" Aimee asked, gesturing at the screen with her chin. "What a dirty dog, lying about shit like that. Hey, whatever happened with the interview with him? You make any progress?"

I prayed she wouldn't spill that I'd been to a ball with him.

Yeah, if progress was a weekend away in his Soho loft and brunch with his parents at their fancy club.

"No. No progress."

"Oh, crap. That's too bad. Well, maybe that will

change now the cat's out of the bag. So to speak. You should call him again. Really."

Aimee was my favorite person at work, but if she didn't shut up soon, I was going to have to punch her.

The news story ended, moving away from delighting in someone's unfortunate fuckup to pressing issues like what the United Nations had on its docket for the day.

People started filing out of the break room, and as they did, I sank into a chair and stared at the floor.

Was it true?

If he really knew the woman accusing him, contrary to his claims, could it also be true he'd knocked her up? I mean, could anything that came out of his mouth be believed at this point?

Poor woman even had photos of the two of them together to prove it.

He'd lied. Plain and simple. And he was not taking responsibility for his actions.

And I'd thought he was a nice guy.

I raced to the ladies' room before the lump in my throat turned to full-on tears.

Fuck, I was supposed to go out with him that night.

Well, scratch that.

I returned to my desk, too shaken to even watch a puppy video. I dialed Bridget.

"Hey, what's up?" she chirped.

"Um, well. Things aren't so good."

A door closed in the background. "Hey, are you at work? Should we talk later?" I asked.

"No, don't worry. I have a couple minutes. Simon and I have used this closet before."

Okay, I really didn't need to know they messed around at work.

"You probably haven't seen the news today, Bridget, but Talbot was on." Shit. The lump on my throat was back. I wanted to smack myself for giving a shit about someone I barely knew, but I also wanted to lie down on the floor and cry because this was just another example of life fucking me.

There I'd been, flying to New York for the weekend on a private plane with a gorgeous man who also happened to be an elected official. And just when I was getting too big for my britches, the universe came along and slapped me down, as if I needed a reminder of my humble beginnings and my unwavering efforts to leave them behind.

"Oh. Well, aren't senators on TV all the time?" she asked.

I sighed. "Yeah, I suppose so. But this story was about him with the woman who has the paternity accusation against him. She had a picture of them together. It proves they knew each other."

She was silent for a moment. "Oh. Shit."

"Yeah," I said quietly.

"Oh, sweetie. I'm sorry. I know you've spent some time with him and even though his parents were pains in the ass, it doesn't feel good to be lied to."

My voice broke. "I don't want anything to do with that creep."

"I don't blame you at all. Look, sweetie, Block Island will be here before you know it, and it will be freaking amazing. We'll go to the beach, cook great dinners, drink good wine, and look at the stars. We'll go sailing and eat lobster. You'll forget about him in no time. In fact, did I tell you? A couple of Simon's buddies from the U.K. will be joining. I've met them, and they're very cute. Their accents are hot as hell."

Bridget was right. Block Island was going to be heavenly. Our long weekend away was coming up in just a few weeks' time, and I needed to keep my eye on that ball. Until then, I'd stay busy at work, and there were loads of new puppies to be tended to at DogHouse. Time would fly by.

But the moment I wrapped up my call with Bridget, my phone buzzed with a text from none other than Talbot.

What fucking nerve. He gets exposed and is ready to get busy with me like nothing ever happened? What was wrong with people like that? No conscience. No sense of responsibility.

what time do you get off work tonight?

Hmmm. I could tell him to go fuck himself. Or I could just lie and say I was no longer available.

Or, I could just not respond. Like a chickenshit.

I dropped my phone into my desk drawer and dug

into the day's top obituary about the founder of the oldest movie theater in D.C.

After I handed in my work to Wayne, I turned my attention to the puppy mill story. I might not have been able to pull off the Talbot interview, but this story was far more important and would be even better than anything I could write about the boy senator. I'd show Ken, and he'd finally see my potential.

But dammit, my thoughts were cluttered with disappointment. Talbot had seemed so sincere, and I'd bought everything he'd said, hook, line, and sinker. What a sucker I was. I'd never learn.

Shortly before quitting time, I brought my article to Ken, who scanned it as I stood there in his office. He was in a hurry to get out the door, probably to rub elbows with some high-ranking official or queen of a small European country, so I took it as a good sign he was reading my stuff even if it was just a quick look.

"So, no luck on the article about Senator Richardson?"

Shit. Did he have to bring that up? I took a deep breath. It wouldn't do to get all weepy with the paper's editor in chief. Everyone already thought those of us in obits were strange, as it was.

I shook my head. "No. No progress on that. I mean,

I've been in touch with him, but he's not granting interviews."

I decided not to tell him I'd spent the weekend with the young senator in his fabulous Soho loft, which didn't result in anything I could write for a newspaper. Maybe *Penthouse* magazine.

He rested on the edge of his desk. "You know, Cricket, you're not the type to easily give up. I can see that. So, if I were you, I'd keep plugging away. Keep asking. He'll eventually have to meet with the press again, and you could be the first in line."

I nodded mutely, wishing he would just focus on the damn puppy story.

"I'll do that, Ken. You're right. I might as well keep my place in line." I laughed to try and seem cool.

But I had to say, Ken's bringing up Talbot was a gut-punch. I'd not considered one of the downsides of being 'friendly' with a public official was that they'd always be in your face in the news or somewhere else, regardless of whether you wanted them to be.

"So, Ken, what about the puppy mill story and Senator Cazzo's legislation? People are really fired up about this issue."

He nodded. "Not sure this is what the paper needs right now, but it's a decent start. I think what might give it teeth is if you went to one of the mills, posing as someone looking to buy a dog."

Oh, hell no. There was no way I was going to look a

bunch of poorly treated dogs in the eyes and just leave them there. I didn't have it in me.

Shit. Shit. Shit.

He must have seen the horror on my face because he continued, "Try digging a little deeper with Cazzo. Why is he sponsoring this legislation? Why does he give a damn? In other words, what is his personal interest? Is there money behind it? That might be a better hook."

Ugh. All that work, and he was only marginally interested.

But he was all over the Talbot story, as if I could do anything about that.

One step forward, two steps back.

"Sounds good. I'll get right on it," I said.

Back at my desk, I realized it was close enough to quitting time that I could pack up my shit and get the hell out of the office. My phone had multiple texts from Talbot.

Delete.

I knew Ken was still counting on me to get an interview, and I'd promised I'd keep trying.

But first, I needed some time to deal with my shit.

I hustled to the Metro. The faster I got to the dog shelter, the better.

It was one place a girl could count on an unconditional warm kiss. Even if it was sloppy and wet.

CHAPTER SIXTEEN

TALBOT

"What the hell is going on?" Damian shouted over my speakerphone.

It's never a good sign when your attorney asks a question like that, but I didn't care. His accusatory tone was pissing me the fuck off.

"Hmmm. Would you like to elaborate?" Yeah, I was in that kind of mood and wasn't above goading him.

He could work for it, since he'd rubbed me the wrong way and exacerbated my already-shit mood.

"Talbot. You *know* what I'm referring to."

If he had a scolding in mind, he'd better save it for another time. I was still pissed that Cricket had ghosted me the night before and blown off our date. I had zero capacity for any more bullshit.

He lowered his voice a notch. "Talbot. Who the hell

is this woman who provided the photo of the two of you together to every press outlet in the free world?"

Someone who was smarter than I was, apparently.

"It was a set-up, Damian. She asked for a photo as Bruce and I were walking over to the Capitol. She seemed normal."

"Bruce was with you? That's good, he can vouch for the photo having been just taken, rather than a year and a half ago as she has claimed. Had you seen her before?"

Shit, I had my photo taken with people all the time.

"I thought about that, and no, I don't think I'd ever seen her."

"Okay. I'm going to have my people run a reverse image search on this woman's photo to see what we can learn about her. If my hunch is right, I suspect it was arranged by Carlotti."

Bastard.

"Can't this all just be resolved with the DNA testing?"

Bruce came barging in. Would that asshole ever learn to knock? "Tal, we gotta head out—" he started.

I gave him the *just a minute signal* and turned my attention back to Damian.

"The woman's story is she shouldn't have to provide any DNA because she *knows* you're the father. Which is a total BS move. She's clearly stalling, probably at the direction of Carlotti. So, I've gotten a court order."

"Jesus Christ," I said.

"Don't worry, Talbot, this will be over soon."

But at what expense?

Bruce and I raced to meet with the other New York members of Congress when I saw Cricket in the distance, talking to Senator Cazzo.

What the hell was she doing here in the Senate building? And why was she talking to him again?

I was barely registering what Bruce was saying. "... and don't forget about that fundraiser tonight at that art collector's house—"

I picked up my speed to see if I could catch Cricket.

"Yo, Tal, I'll catch you later then?" he called after me, giving up.

But before I could get close enough to call to her, she took off around a corner, and Cazzo headed in my direction, stopping me.

"Well, the young Senator Richardson," he said with a big grin, "guess you're having quite the day, aren't you?"

Ugh. The last person I wanted to get stuck talking to.

He put his hand on my arm, trapping me.

"Say, how are your parents with all this paternity stuff? Your mother must be apoplectic."

I laughed, when I really would have liked to punch the smug look off his face.

"Oh, you know my mother. She lives for drama."

And he did know her, at least as well as anyone knew her from the country club and charity circuit. Cripes, I wasn't even certain I knew my mother very well. She had a hide as tough as they came, rarely letting on what she was really thinking in order to cultivate the image she'd always felt she deserved—that of an attractive, wealthy politician's wife.

I got it—she was adapting to the world she lived in. She really had no choice. As exclusive as her circle was, if anyone was shunned or kicked out of it, they pretty much had nowhere else to go.

"Hey, Senator Cazzo, do you mind if I ask you what you were talking to Cricket Curtain about?"

He raised an eyebrow. "I don't mind at all. She's doing some sort of write-up on my puppy mill bill. You know that issue. Something about the inhumane conditions dogs are bred in. It's a terrible thing, really." He waved his hand dismissively.

Oh right.

He raised an eyebrow. "Are you interested in her? Why are you asking?"

I shrugged. "Oh, I went to college with her. I see her around from time to time. Didn't know she was covering the political beat."

That shit-eating smile spread across his face again. "I don't know what beat she's covering, but she's always welcome in my office, if you know what I mean."

Shit.

"Uh, I don't know what you mean."

He looked around to make sure no one could hear us. "Have you seen the tits on that girl? Christ, my dick gets hard every time I talk to her. And I'm sixty-five years old. It takes a lot to get me hard—"

I help my hands up. "I don't really need to hear this—"

But he didn't stop. "She's a great-looking woman. I was thinking of asking her to dinner. Strictly business, as you can imagine."

He winked slowly.

Fuck if I wasn't beginning to hate this man more than I thought I could. I didn't like him talking about Cricket that way. I didn't like him talking about *any* woman that way.

"You know, one night when Mrs. Cazzo is out at Bridge or some other stupid activity, I might have a little personal time with our sweet Cricket. What do you think? Do you think she'd go for it? Was she a typical college slut? Because I really like that sort of—"

"I gotta go, Senator," I said loudly, slapping him on the back.

A bit too hard.

He stumbled forward and coughed, frowning at me.

"Got a meeting with a bunch of New Yorkers. See ya later."

I took off before I decked the asshole.

Seriously. Him with Cricket? I knew that would never happen, but for him to even consider it was an insult of massive fucking proportion.

The meeting with the New York gang was a complete bust from my perspective. I was too rattled by Cazzo's trash-talk and by the curious looks I was getting from everyone in the meeting, likely due to the newest development in my baby daddy problem.

In fact, I could barely string together a coherent sentence, that's how fucked up I was. Fortunately, a lot of people in the room were folks I'd known for a long time. I knew they'd cut me slack.

I also knew Damian was working on my case, but I was getting seriously impatient.

And just as I was cursing him in my head, my phone buzzed.

"Damian," I said in a hushed tone as I moved to a quiet corner.

"Talbot. Are you somewhere you can talk?" He sounded out of breath.

"Yeah. What's going on?"

He released a big breath. Either this was going to be very good or very bad.

And I hoped it was good because I couldn't take any more fucking shit for one day.

"Just heard from my PI. The woman is recanting her story."

I lowered myself to the closest chair and put my head in my hand, waiting for my latest migraine to explode. "Are you fucking kidding me? It's over?"

I could hear the smile in his voice. The man loved nothing more than victory. "It seems so, Talbot."

I could hardly believe it.

"Well, what the hell happened?" I asked.

"I can't go into detail because I don't have a lot of detail—when I work with my PI, it's often the less he tells me, the better—but from what I know, when she found out she could be facing prison time for committing a felony, she changed her tune fast."

Holy fucking shit. This didn't mean all my problems were gone, but it did mean a pretty fucking huge one was. I still had to deal with the fallout, but things were sure as hell looking up.

"And I'm pretty sure we'll be able to pin this on Carlotti."

Fuck yeah.

"I gotta run," Damian said, "but do me a favor, Talbot."

"What's that?"

"Keep it in your pants. You don't need something like this cropping up again. It would ruin your career. And if you can't keep it in your pants, which you seem to have trouble with, be careful who you whip it out for."

I swiped my phone closed.

The man might have been my family attorney for more years than I could remember, but he wasn't going to tell me how to run my life.

Or who I could fuck.

This time, I was the one barging into Bruce's office for a change. Our press secretary sat opposite him, and he was dazzling her with some stupid story. God, what the guy wouldn't do for some female attention.

If he weren't such a good political operative, I'd have him out on his ass. Best friend notwithstanding.

"Hey, you mind if I have a few minutes with Bruce, here?" I asked her.

"Sure!"

Bruce's gaze was fixed to her ass as she tottered out on some very high heels.

"Dude, you'd better not be fucking her."

He rolled his eyes. I knew what that meant.

He wasn't fucking her. But he *planned* to.

Whatever. He could deal with his own shit if he ended up in it.

I shook off my irritation. I'd just received good news and I wasn't going to let my horn dog chief of staff ruin it.

"Bruce, just got a call from Damian. The woman backed off her story."

His mouth fell open for a moment before he slammed his hand on his desk and jumped out of his chair. "Fucking A, Tal. That is seriously good news. *Yes.*" He paced the office, clapping his hands together.

"Guess you can talk to the press again," he said, slapping me on the back. "I'll have Rose call Anderson Cooper."

"Yeah, Bruce you do that."

I headed back to my own office, ready to call another important media person I needed to meet with.

The intercom on my desk squawked with the voice of my admin. "I've got the call placed for you, Senator."

I lunged for the phone just as the call was transferred.

"Washington Chronicle, Cricket Curtain speaking."

Yes.

I cleared my throat. "Cricket, it's Talbot."

She was silent for a moment and then sighed.

Not a good sign.

"Hi, Talbot."

Jesus.

"Cricket, I've been trying to get in touch with you. And what the hell about last night?"

Fuck, she wasn't making it easy. I took a deep breath to temper my frustration. I wasn't usually one to chase after a woman. In fact, I never chased women, but damn, if she was ghosting me, I wanted to know why.

"Sorry. Been super busy," she said.

Okay, there was something up her ass, no question.

"Cricket, I wanted to let you know I can do interviews now. I thought I'd give you first crack. My press embargo is over."

There was going to be a backlog of media requests, but there was no one I'd rather start with than a beautiful redhead.

"Oh, thanks. I'm on to something else now. In fact, I need to get back to work."

The line went dead.

Well, fuck me.

I sat for a second, just staring at the receiver in my hand. Then, I realized what I had to do. I grabbed my jacket and headed out.

"Senator, are you off to a meeting?" Evelyn asked.

"Sort of," I told her.

In front of the Senate building, I waved down a cab.

"Washington Chronicle, please," I told him.

The cabbie raced across fifteen blocks or so, and when I got to the newspaper offices, I walked to the front desk.

"I'm here to see Cricket Curtain."

A bored young woman looked up and in seconds, her eyes widened with recognition.

"Senator Richardson?" she asked.

I nodded, desperate to contain my impatience.

"I saw you on the news today," she said, as if I might not be aware.

I didn't have the heart to tell her half the world had seen me on the news.

"Um. Let me go get Cricket for you." She dashed

through a set of locked double doors that I managed to put my foot in before they closed.

The receptionist, unaware I was on her tail, hustled through the office.

Heads started popping up from behind cubicle walls, and a murmur spread through the crowd.

"Senator Richardson!" someone called to me.

The receptionist turned around and stopped, horrified I'd followed her into the office without having been invited.

So, I had to stop, too.

A guy with glasses jogged up behind me. "Senator. What a nice surprise to see you here in the paper's office. Can we help you with something?"

All work stopped as everyone stared.

Guess they didn't get a lot of senators barging into their offices.

"I'm here for Cricket Curtain," I said.

Confusion crossed his face. "Cricket Curtain? You must be mistaken. Are you sure you aren't wanting to see somebody else with the paper?" he asked with a little laugh.

"Why wouldn't I be here for Cricket?"

He stepped toward me, holding his hands up like he was trying to reason. "Well, she's just in obituaries. Unless you need an obituary written?" He laughed and patted my back like we were buds.

I tried not to smirk. "No, I don't need an obituary written. Thanks, though."

I turned, hoping the receptionist would continue walking.

"Sir," he said, putting his hand on my arm to stop me, "can I take you to see one of our more seasoned writers? Or maybe the editor in chief, Ken Brady?"

Really? A 'more seasoned' writer? What a dick. I maneuvered my arm out of his grip, irritation creeping up the back of my neck.

I stepped closer to him, lowering my voice. "Look. I told you I'm here to see Cricket. That's all you need to know. So, I'd like you to ease up on the questions and leave me be."

His head snapped back. "Sure, Senator. Go right ahead."

He nodded at the receptionist, who continued through the maze of beige cubes, until we reached one in the far corner.

"Hello Cricket."

CHAPTER SEVENTEEN

CRICKET

Talbot Richardson leaned against my cube wall, arms crossed, wearing a half-smile and one of his incredible suits.

"What are you doing here?" I asked.

That sexy half-smile.

The one I had been trying to forget.

Run sister, run.

Too much drama, too much baggage. I mean, he'd denied impregnating some woman, then she said she had proof, and next, she dropped the whole thing.

These people belonged in crazy town.

And now, he's showing up in my office?

What the hell?

But it didn't matter. I didn't need his kind of bullshit

in my life. Thank god he'd never noticed me at college. So much better that way.

I peeked over my cube wall and saw the receptionist practically running back to the safety of her own desk.

That explained how he'd gotten this far.

"I wanted to talk to you," he said, running his hand through his thick black hair.

"Talbot, I have a call scheduled—" I looked at the time on my computer, "—right now. I can't talk."

Fuck, I wanted him to leave, and I didn't want him to leave. I hated myself for that.

Embarrassment washed over me as his eyes scanned my messy cube. He'd know I was the lowly little drone that I was. Just a nobody writer who got little to no respect. Actually, maybe he'd always known that and felt sorry for me. And that filled me with shame, the same kind of shame that my fear of falling on my ass and having to move back to Rhode Island filled me with.

I wanted to go home and slide beneath the covers. Pull them up over my eyes. Not be an adult for as long as I could. Puppy videos weren't enough to help me out of this one.

"I'll wait," he said, moving a stack of keyboards off an unsteady office chair. He pulled out his phone and opened what looked like the New York Times, unbothered by a thing.

That was the problem with people like him. They weren't bothered by much because life had granted them the world's biggest safety nets. One profession doesn't work out? Just try another. One relationship doesn't work out? Find a new one.

Connections, money, and the universe smiling down on them.

Everything I didn't have and never would.

He gestured toward my phone with his chin. "Go ahead. Take your call." When I didn't move, he looked up from his phone. "I have some reading to catch up on. Don't mind me."

Don't mind me. Was he fucking kidding? I *did* mind him. I minded him being in my cube, and I minded him being in my life.

But I was already late for a call with the widow of the recently deceased man who had invented some sort of quick-charging battery.

And once I was done with that call, I planned to put the finishing touches on my puppy mill story. If Ken wasn't dazzled by it—well, I didn't know what I'd do.

I put my headset on and dialed. "Mrs. Waltz, it's Cricket Curtain from the Washington Chronicle. I'm so sorry for your loss... "

I chatted with Mrs. Waltz for fifteen minutes as she gave me some background on her husband's personal and professional life, as well as the invention he was famous for.

"You take good care of yourself, Mrs. Waltz. Thank you."

Hanging up the phone, I took a deep breath. It wasn't easy talking to people who'd just lost a loved one, never mind asking them a shit ton of questions about the person.

"You handled that with a lot of compassion."

Christ, I'd forgotten he was there.

"Thank you. Now, don't you have some senator kind of business to attend to?"

He leaned closer and lowered his voice. "What the fuck, Cricket? What the hell is going on?"

"Nothing's going on. Nothing was ever going on. We had a—"

Wayne appeared in the doorway to my cube.

"Hello," he said to Talbot. I was quite sure he had no idea who he was.

He turned to me. "How'd that interview with Mrs. Waltz go?"

"Great, Wayne. I'm gonna write it up right now." I looked at Talbot. "Well, as soon as I'm free to do so."

Wayne looked between the two of us and with a blank face, returned to his own cube.

Talbot stood. "C'mon." He grabbed my arm and pulled me to my feet. "I want to talk to you, and I want to talk right now. Where can we go for some privacy?"

I just looked at him. I both wanted and didn't want to hear what he had to say.

He looked around. "Is that a closet over there?"

I nodded.

"Let's go."

Once inside, he pulled the door closed behind us in a room that smelled of number two pencils and reams of printer paper. I saw an old umbrella in the corner that was mine, which I'd thought was lost.

Some fucker had borrowed it and not had the balls to give it back to me directly. Asshole.

Talbot leaned against an empty rack. "Cricket, at one time, interviewing me was pretty high on your agenda. I know what it means to your career. And I'm sure you know that the woman who accused me has recanted her story. I can talk to the press again, and I want to start with you."

He was wearing me down. Actually, he'd been wearing me down since he'd shown up at my cube.

But I would resist.

He looked at his watch. "I have to get back. Meet me for lunch in one hour at The Monocle. You know where it is."

And he left me in the closet with my old umbrella.

"Bridg," I said breathlessly.

Yes, I was running to the Metro, to meet Talbot for lunch on Capitol Hill.

"Jesus. Are you running marathons now?" she asked.

I dodged a group of school kids on their way to a White House tour, and stopped at the entrance to the Farragut North Metro station before I lost my cell connection.

"Sorry, running for the Metro. So, you know Talbot, right?"

A door closed in the background. Was she in the same closet where she and Simon—

Never mind, I didn't want to think about that.

"Oh, my god, I saw on the news that the whole baby daddy thing was BS, just like he told you."

I swallowed hard to ward off choking up.

"Crick, are you there? Are you okay?"

"Bridget, he just showed up at my office and demanded I meet him for lunch."

Cripes, why hadn't I worn a better dress and shoes that day?

"He showed up at your office? Are you fucking kidding me? Holy shit. That's so sweet."

Ugh. She'd just pushed me over the edge, and the tears started to flow, right there on the corner of Connecticut and K Streets.

God, I was a fucking loser.

"Cricket, why are you crying? What the hell is going on?"

I sniffled. "We're not right for each other. First, there were his snobby parents, and then, this paternity scandal. I would have to deal with that shit *all the time* if I continued hanging out with him."

She sighed loudly. "*Hanging out?* You've done more than hang out with that guy. You spent a freaking weekend with him."

"That's why I have to put a stop to anything further."

"I don't get you, Cricket. He's not perfect. He has baggage—but show me one person who doesn't. I mean, are you that perfect? Is your life that perfect?"

"He's offered to let me interview him for the paper."

"Are you fucking kidding me? What are you waiting for? This could be your big break."

Something beeped angrily in the background. "Shit. I'm being paged. I'll call ya later, sweetie. Don't throw the baby out with the bath water. Just don't."

I swiped my phone closed and ran down the escalator to catch the train coming into the station. I wedged myself into a crowded car and reached to hold the bar above my head as the train sped toward Capitol Hill.

CHAPTER EIGHTEEN

TALBOT

I sipped my scotch.

Cricket sat directly across from me, looking around The Monocle, a venerable Capitol Hill institution that catered to the city's movers and shakers. It was one of the few places I could go where I wouldn't turn heads, at least not too many. I was a pissant in this crowd of folks who'd been in Congress way longer than I had, and I was fine with that.

After a couple lobbyists stopped by our table to say hello, Cricket fished a notebook out of her bag but kept it in her lap.

She leaned toward me over the table. "I don't want to make it obvious to everyone that I'm interviewing you. People are so nosy."

I looked around and noticed at least a couple ears cocked in our direction.

"That's fine. Put your phone on the table and record us. No one will realize you're doing that."

She shrugged, her dark eyes scanning back and forth.

Christ, she should have been a spy.

She pushed her red hair behind her shoulders and rummaged in her bag for her phone. She tapped its screen a few times and set it on the table.

"We're recording, now." She glanced at the notebook in her lap.

"Okay, Miss Curtain. Fire away," I said, smiling.

She took a gulp of the ice water she'd ordered. "Okay then. What's it like to be the youngest elected senator in history?"

"Well," I said, leaning over the table so the recording would be clear, "it's exciting. Although sometimes, I feel a little out of my element, but isn't everyone like that with a new job?"

She nodded slowly.

"I'm working with people who are for the most part a lot older than I. I need to earn their respect as quickly as I can. That's why I'm so grateful the paternity accusations against me have been resolved. Who was going to take me seriously with something like that hanging over my head? You know what I'm saying, Miss Curtain?"

Her eyes widened, just like I knew they would. She hadn't expected me to go for the elephant in the room.

But I didn't see a reason why I shouldn't. I needed to clear the air. And sanitize it, too.

She glanced at her pad again, resisting the urge to start scribbling. "Did you always want to be in politics and follow in your father's footsteps?"

"No."

Again, her eyes widened. Yeah, I was more honest than the old guard politicians, who would have had rehearsed canned answers for anything anyone could think to ask them.

I could hear it now: *Why yes, I've wanted to be in elected office ever since I was president of my kindergarten class...*

I wouldn't put it past any of them.

Cricket raced through her list of questions while nibbling on a shrimp cocktail. I had ordered a big, rare steak and a baked potato.

I'd never had an interview that the journalist wanted to get over with so fast.

"What are your top issues?" she asked.

I resisted the attempt to be a smart ass. Well, mostly resisted.

"You probably know, Miss Curtain, that the environment is my passion. But I also have an eye to abolishing puppy mills."

A pink blush washed over her face, and I'll be

damned if it wasn't one of the hottest things I'd ever seen in my life.

My dick twitched as I imagined taking her into the restaurant's bathroom, bending her over the sink, and—

"Senator? Senator, are you listening?" she asked.

Shit.

"Yes. Sorry. Was lost in thought for a moment," I said.

I flicked off the recorder on her phone and reached for her hand.

She looked around nervously, but I didn't care who saw me.

"Cricket, there's another reason I wanted you to meet me for lunch today, aside from answering your interview questions."

She slowly pulled her hand out of mine.

"And it wasn't just to learn more about puppy mills."

A slight smile crossed her beautiful face.

"Now that we've got business out of the way, I'd like to take you—"

She stood, bumping the table and knocking over her glass of water.

"I... I can't... I need to go..." She grabbed her bag off the back of her chair.

She took off, forgetting her phone on the table.

I turned to call her, but she'd run for the door and was gone. I picked up the phone, wiped off the splotches of water she'd spilled on it, and dropped it into my pocket.

"Senator Cazzo," I called, running to catch up to the old man once I was back in the Senate Building.

He turned around, his lined face and white hair giving him the perfect 'elder statesman' look.

"Hey, Talbot, congrats on the outcome of the paternity matter. Say, I heard you had a great fundraiser last week."

Fuck if gossip didn't travel fast in the halls of the Senate. I was going to have to speak with my staff about confidentiality.

"Thank you. Just coming from lunch at The Monocle."

"Oh yes, an old favorite of mine. Glad to know the younger generation is enjoying the iconic restaurant."

Christ, he even *sounded* senatorial.

"Hey, I have a couple questions about your puppy mill bill."

He frowned. "Why are you so interested in that? Wait, I know! You've got a thing for that lovely little filly. What was her name again?"

He put his finger on his temple and tapped, trying to remember.

"Are you thinking of Cricket Curtain, the woman from the Washington Chronicle?" I asked.

Eyes widening, he grinned lasciviously. "Yes, I think so. Was she the one with the big—"

"I'd appreciate your not talking about her that way—"

"So, the boy does have a thing for the lovely miss. But I tell you what, if you don't want her, Talbot, just let me know. I'll make my move so fast she won't know what hit her."

My stomach churned, all the worse for the gluttonous lunch I'd just inhaled.

He leaned closer to me. "Young man, are you fucking her? Because you honestly should be. Don't be a fool and miss the opportunities being a senator drops in your lap."

I was gonna kill him.

He continued. "And about the goddamn puppy mill bill, or whatever it's called. You think I give a shit about puppy mills?" He waved his hand dismissively. "I sponsored this to shut up one of those pain-in-the ass interest groups. Well, also because it will look good on my record next to all the defense spending I'm supporting. Imagine that, will you? I want to double the Pentagon's budget but also save the nation's puppies."

He leaned toward me, shaking with silent laughter.

Despicable dirt bag. He tried to touch my arm, but I recoiled. I didn't want to lose my lunch right there in the hallway.

Were all the members of Congress like this asshole?

Had my father been like him?

I took a step toward Cazzo, as if I were going to

whisper something in his hear. He met me halfway, clearly hoping for something dirty and confidential.

When his ear was inches from my mouth, I stepped forward onto the shiny black wingtip shoe he wore and ground my sharp heel into the top of his foot.

Grabbing his arm, I whispered, "If I ever hear you talk again like that about Cricket, or any other woman, I won't step on your foot, Senator. I'll be stepping on your throat."

I shoved him just enough to bounce off the wall behind him.

"What? How dare you—"

I leaned in his face again. "What about my threat did you not understand?"

He pressed his lips tightly and narrowed his eyes. But he kept his big mouth shut for once.

Was I supposed to spend the next six years of my life with people like him? Was this the best Washington had to offer?

Fuck this town.

Back in my office, I popped two migraine pills and leaned back, resting my head.

As soon as the pain began to subside, I called my parents.

"Hi, Mom."

She sucked in her breath. "Oh, Talbot..."

I sat up straight in my chair. "Mom? Is something wrong?"

"No..." she sniffled.

"Mom, why are you crying?"

She blew her nose. "It's just that... that I was so excited about becoming a grandmother."

Holy fucking shit. That's what she was weeping about?

"Mom, you *wanted* that woman to have gotten pregnant by me? Are you *kidding*?"

I struggled to keep my voice in check, but it wasn't helping. After all I'd gone through, including her having scolded me about the whole thing, she actually wanted it to be true?

Jesus fucking Christ.

"Well, Talbot, would it really have been so bad...?"

"Mom, put Dad on the line please."

"Son, great news!" my father said immediately.

"I know, Dad. Thank you for your support on all this. It hasn't been easy."

He chuckled. "Nothing worth having is easy. Isn't that right?"

Did they teach these platitudes in 'Senate School?' Because these people were all starting to sound alike.

"Hey, my PI just called with some additional news," my father said. "Carlotti was indeed behind the accusation. The woman has fled to Europe, probably with the money he paid her, but he can't leave the country.

They're taking the whole thing to the District Attorney tomorrow. We may be able to press charges for slander."

Had the wind just been knocked out of me? Because it sure felt like it.

"It's just incredible what people will do to each other, either to get ahead, or for revenge. If this is the way it's done, I don't want any part of it," I said.

In spite of the pills I'd just taken, my migraine continued to circle.

"Talbot, there are bad actors wherever you go. You'll learn not to let them get under your skin. Give it time."

"Yeah. Right. Hey, I'll talk to you later. Oh, and get Mom to chill out."

"Oh no. I'm staying out of the line of fire on that one."

I got Cricket on the phone on the first ring.

"Thank you for joining me for lunch," I said.

"Thank *you*. And thank you for the interview. I apologize about my rudeness and running out. I have a lot on my mind," she said. "And I left my phone there, didn't I?"

"Yup. I have it."

I cleared my throat so I didn't sound like I was calling bullshit. "Hey, I was serious about wanting to know more about puppy mills. I... have a feeling I can

take it further than Cazzo. Let's just say his commitment is questionable."

"Really? I thought he was so passionate about it."

The only thing that man was passionate about was
getting into Cricket's panties. I promised myself that,
next time I saw my father, I'd fill him in on what a creep
his friend was. He might not believe me or choose to do
anything about it, but at least I could say I'd
warned him.

Unless he was just like him?

"Eh. Let's just say he has a lot of commitments."

How was that for diplomacy?

"Well, what would you like to know about the mills?
You could come by the DogHouse shelter and I could
show you some of the pups we've rescued from them."

I hadn't even thought about that. "That sounds
great. But I'd like to see you tonight."

Fuck, I'd just seen her. But I wanted to see her
again. I had to.

This was unfamiliar territory for me, this longing. I
didn't understand it, except that I needed it. I
needed *her*.

"Um. Okay. I guess I could do that. Get together
tonight."

"Awesome. Why don't you come over for a glass of
wine around seven? If we're hungry, we can order pizza.
And don't worry, you don't have to take notes this
time."

CHAPTER NINETEEN

CRICKET

Seriously.

Talbot Richardson was *working* it. I wasn't too stupid to see that.

He took me to a nice lunch, gave me first dibs on an interview, and now was inviting me over for drinks.

And to think, just a few years earlier, I'd followed him around our college campus like a little puppy dog.

Something he'd *never* know.

Just like he'd never know I'd faked an injury to meet him.

Funny how things come full circle. Or not.

I couldn't deny I was dying to see him and have him devour me the way he had on our weekend in New York. But on the other hand, the sensible side of me was screaming *Run! Run the other way!*

What could possibly come out of spending time together? He needed to be with sophisticated, glamorous society girls like his friend Halliday.

He needed a woman like her, whom his bitchy mother would approve of. He needed someone who knew how to play the D.C. game, where if you overhear someone talking shit about you in a ladies' room, you know just how to handle it.

I was an obits girl, and an obits girl I would remain. In fact, I'd bet that after I turned in my little story about Talbot, Ken would pat me on the head and send me right back to my cube.

He wasn't interested in advancing me. He just wanted his damn story about the boy senator.

But in spite of the clear signals that my life was going nowhere, I was still going over Talbot's for some wine and a make-out session. Fucking A, I wasn't *that* proud.

Of course, I'd had to act like I didn't know where he lived. It wouldn't do to tip him off that I'd stalked him in the early days of trying to get my story.

I'd just never planned on his being interested in me. Or so nice. And kind. And a volunteer.

So, I dutifully pretended to jot down his address. "How's the parking over there?" I asked to make myself sound legit.

"Pretty hard. Pull into the space behind my house."

He had a parking spot? No one in D.C. had a parking spot. At least not anyone *I* knew. They were like unicorns, personal parking spaces. I was never sure whether they really, actually existed.

On the drive over, I told myself repeatedly I'd stay for one or two glasses of wine. That was it. Okay, and maybe a little make out session. But that was *really* it. No need to start something that could never end well.

"Hey, gorgeous," he said when he opened the door in his shirtsleeves and trousers. I spotted a suit jacket and tie thrown over a chair in the corner.

Okay. Maybe I'd stay longer than just a little make out session.

I slipped the sweater off my shoulders and dropped it on the bench in the foyer.

"Wow," I said, looking around, "this place is so different from your New York loft."

He nodded with a grimace. "I know. It's not my style, not at all. But it will have to do for now. It was furnished, so I didn't have to move much down here."

I followed him into the galley kitchen, through a very traditional hallway and dining room.

I tried to sound positive. "Um. It's not so bad. You know, you could paint or something."

He handed me a glass of wine. "Eh. Not worth it. I'm just renting, and the next tenant might be in love with this colonial bullshit."

He moved closer to me, and my heart began to slam against my chest. "Cheers," he murmured and leaned down to kiss me, pressing me against the kitchen counter.

Damn him.

His wine-scented lips brushed over mine, and in seconds, one of his hands was on my waist with the other burrowed in my hair. I hadn't even noticed him put his wine down.

"Come with me."

He grabbed his glass and took me by the hand.

I followed him into the living room, which was just as traditional as the rest of the house, and we settled into an overstuffed floral chintz sofa.

I ran my hand over the faded cotton. "Wow. Laura Ashley called. She wants her dress back."

He laughed. "Hey now. No need to make it worse. As it is, every day I come home I feel like I'm in my grandmother's house."

"Well, the wine is good." The warm feeling I always got from my first couple sips washed over me, and I began to relax. The room grew toasty, and I pulled my hair forward over one shoulder to cool my neck.

I found Talbot staring at me, and I involuntarily shifted in my seat. Apparently, my resolve had not only dissolved, but it had also left me high and dry.

He reached to play with a piece of my hair, twirling it around his finger.

"Thank you for the interview today. I wrote most of it up and plan to submit a draft to my editor tomorrow."

He nodded slowly. "Let me know if you need anything else. I'm an open book."

I studied him. "I suppose you are. Why don't you

tell me why you are suddenly so interested in puppy mills?"

I could tell he was choosing his words carefully. Such a politician. "I get the feeling from talking to Senator Cazzo that his plate is, um, full, like I said. He might not have the time he needs to put into this."

Well, that wasn't good news. "Crap. I know I'm supposed to be objective and all, but I was really rooting for this."

"Tell me more."

I set my glass down. "Here's the thing. It's perfectly legal to breed dogs. Some people do it in their homes, and some do it in huge commercial kennels. Where things get sketchy is when the animals are neglected or treated inhumanely. You know, like if they're not given enough food or water, shelter from the elements, or the medical care they might need. It can happen anywhere, but it mostly happens in the places that sell through large pet stores."

The more I talked about it, the more pissed I got, too. Her enthusiasm was infectious.

"And what does the proposed legislation do?" he asked.

"Good question. It imposes standards on anyone who raises animals for resale. It also gives the states grants and the authority to set up inspections."

His eyebrows rose. "Holy shit. You really know your stuff."

There was that sexy half-smile again.

Fuck me.

"Thank you. It's simple legislation, but sometimes, simple is all you need."

He stood and extended his hand. "We're going upstairs."

Huh?

"That's kind of presumptuous, don't you think?"

"Absolutely," he said, his eyes twinkling dangerously.

Cripes. I couldn't have said no if I'd wanted to.

I took his hand and followed him up some thickly carpeted steps into a dimly lit, sparsely decorated room.

I gripped my wine glass so he wouldn't see my hands shaking.

"How come this room doesn't look like the others?" I asked.

He pressed a remote control, and the sounds of Billie Holiday filled the room.

"The rest of the house was traditional enough, without sleeping in a room of the same. I had everything moved out of this one bedroom, except for what I absolutely needed." He looked around. "It's a little more to my taste, don't you think?"

It was hard to tell in the dim light, and besides, I wasn't really focused on the décor. Talbot stood at the other side of the room from me and began to unbutton his cuffs. When he'd finished with the front of his shirt, he untucked it from his trousers and threw it aside.

And there he was. The same delicious hard body I'd drooled over in New York and dreamt of every night since. I wanted to say no. To run out the door. But my feet were frozen in place.

The bottom line was, I may have wanted to split, but I wanted *him* more.

He approached me, and when he was so close I could feel his breath, he took my wine glass and set it aside. Again, he ran his hands through my hair, scooping handfuls to his face and inhaling deeply. He took a long strand and ran it through his thumb and forefinger, studying it like it was something other-worldly.

Returning his gaze to mine, he twirled a strand around his finger again, and when it was taut, he pulled on it to maneuver my face toward his.

As if I were on a leash.

His mouth crashed into mine, and I waited for his tongue. His free hand opened my jeans, and in seconds, his fingers slipped down my panties to zero in on my clit.

I opened his belt and fly, letting his pants drop to the floor. Easing his boxers below his ass, and my hand flew to his erection, throbbing and wet at the tip.

Without even thinking, I dropped to my knees and licked the length of his shaft.

He gazed down at me, his expression stern. As I guided him into my mouth, he gripped my head and pushed his hips into my face.

I took him until he hit the back of my throat and felt a flood between my legs when he groaned in loud satisfaction. With my hand on the root of his cock, I cradled his balls in my other, closing for a firm grip.

"Fuck, baby, your mouth feels good," he grunted.

He grabbed my shoulders and pulled me to standing, leaving his cock bouncing between us and my mouth hanging open.

"Get up on the bed," he said, gesturing with his chin.

My jeans hanging open, I sat on the edge, wondering what he had in mind.

"No. Get on your knees on the bed."

Oh.

When I'd done so, he yanked my jeans below my ass and ran the inside of his hands through my soaked folds. I gasped and squirmed, pushing back in a silent bid for more.

"Head down," he growled, pulling my cheeks open and running his tongue from my ass to my clit.

My face was pressed into the mattress at an angle that gave me just enough room to breathe. It didn't, however, allow me to see what was going on behind me. A drawer next to the bed slid open, followed by the tear of a foil packet, and snapping of rubber.

He returned, his lips next to my ear. "You good, baby? You want me to fuck you a little? Because I will, but only if you want me to."

I started to raise my head. "Yes—"

But he pressed it down again. Not enough so I couldn't breathe, but enough that I couldn't move.

He notched himself at my opening, my jeans still circling my thighs, and reached to stroke my back.

Slowly easing in, he gave me time to adjust to his girth. The crazy thing was, that before he was even deep inside, I started to come.

I eased back on him, and when I'd grabbed the sheets for purchase, began to buck against him so that he didn't even have to move to fuck me. I pounded the bed with my fists and rocked back on his cock, coming until I heard him holler through his own orgasm. He squeezed his fingers into my hips, gripping me so deeply, it hurt.

But I didn't care.

I woke up some time in the night. It was pitch dark, and Talbot was breathing deeply next to me, a sure sign he was down for the count.

I didn't know why, but my heart was pounding and I was drenched in sweat. I slipped out of bed, grabbed my clothes, and tiptoed downstairs.

What the hell was I doing?

Had he lured me over by faking interest in puppy mills to get into my pants? Because if he had, it had worked.

What a fucking idiot I was.

~

I didn't usually spend my Saturdays at the DogHouse,

but I needed to do something that would clear my mind. A little puppy love never hurt anyone.

As soon as I'd tethered three little charges, I loaded up with biodegradable poop bags and we set out. Like always, the pups were too young to grasp the concept of walking in a straight line, so it took about twenty minutes to reach the end of the block and come back. Which was fine—it was all they needed and about all I could take of them attempting to gobble up anything small enough to fit in their tiny mouths—rocks, acorns, garbage, you name it.

Of course, I ambled extra slowly past the entrance to the community center. I didn't know whether Talbot did his coaching thing on the weekends, but I was drawn to see what was going on inside a place that seemed so important to him.

I walked toward the gym, following the bounce and squeak of basketballs, and first saw all the little boys running up and down the court, dribbling, two at a time.

And, I saw Talbot.

Fuck.

Fortunately, he hadn't seen me. I ducked out of sight and began to steer the pups back out on the sidewalk.

But curiosity got the better of me, and I eased back toward the gym, hoping the dogs wouldn't give me away.

I stayed out of view and just inside the door, I could hear Talbot having a talk with one of the kids.

"Things are getting hard at home, are they?" he asked.

I heard sniffles.

"Uh-huh," an upset little person said.

"Want to tell me what's going on?"

"My mom and dad got in a fight. They were yelling really bad."

Oh, god. My heart broke for this kid.

"Wow. I'm sorry to hear that," Talbot said. "I'd be upset, too. You want a hug?"

More sniffles. "Yeah."

I peeked around the corner to see Talbot squatting to the height of his young charge, his arms wrapped tightly around him.

And he was stroking the little guy's back.

Damn if my heart didn't melt, that he cared enough to comfort a kid who probably felt like his whole world was falling apart.

"You feel a little better, now?" he asked.

"Y... yes, Mister Senator. Thank you."

"Ready to re-join practice? Or would you rather take a break and watch for a bit?"

I peeked again and found Talbot holding the child's hand as they walked back toward the group.

"I'm ready to play, now."

Just as Talbot said "Awesome!" he turned and caught me spying.

Oops.

Surprise washed over his face, and he turned to the kids.

"Excuse me, guys." He escorted the little guy back into the group and then jogged over to me.

The kids were making their usual catcalls in the background.

He stood right in front of me and tilted his head, staring me down. After a moment, he said, "Meet me back here when you're done with the dogs."

And he ran back to the kids. He didn't wait for my answer. He didn't have to.

He knew I'd be there.

CHAPTER TWENTY

TALBOT

The bounce of a basketball echoed in the empty gym, where one last kid was trying for one more basket while waiting for his ride home.

I took a seat in the bleachers where Cricket was waiting. "You ran off this morning. Or was it in the middle of the night?" I asked.

She sighed. "Yeah, I did. I... I just needed to go home."

I straddled the bleacher seat so I could face her. She was looking down, her thick red hair shielding her face.

What was up with that?

I placed my fingers on her chin and turned her face toward mine.

"I'm sorry," she said, looking at me from under her heavy fringe of eyelashes.

"It's okay."

"Why are you here on a Saturday?" she asked.

I wanted to ask why she'd come to the community center, looking for me. But, I didn't.

"We have two extra practices before the season starts," I said, waving at the last kid to get picked up.

She nodded. "Oh. I see."

"Hey, I need to get something at the office. Why don't you come with me and then we'll get some lunch?"

I extended my hand, and she took it, only letting go long enough to get in the car, where she held it all the way across town.

"Wow. Very senatorial," she said, walking around my office.

Her short dress swung back and forth over her ass, bringing me back to our fun of the night before.

And now, I was getting hard, goddammit.

She stopped before the window that provided a perfect view of the Capitol Building.

"What a beautiful sight."

I walked over and put my arms around her, my fingers landing on her full tits. I ground my cock into her backside, grateful it was a Saturday and that no one else was in the office.

But I'd locked the door behind us, anyway.

"Yeah, I got lucky with this office. They usually give the shitty ones on the first floor to the newbies."

She seemed to appreciate that we had the place to ourselves, too. Leaning back, she ground her ass into my aching crotch. "What are you doing?" she asked.

I ran my lips up the side of her neck. "I'm surprised you feel the need to ask. Do you mean what *am I doing in this moment*, or are you asking in a broader way?"

She spun around, dislodging my hands from her breasts.

My cock pressed painfully against the restriction of my blue jeans. Fuck, I was in need of some relief.

"I guess in the broader way."

I pressed my lips to hers. I knew she had a question, but I couldn't help myself.

My tongue swept across her lips, and I watched her eyes flutter closed. I moved my mouth next to her ear.

"I want you. I want you in my life."

There. I'd said it.

She looked up at me and tilted her head. A slow smile spread across her face.

"And what do *you* want?" I asked. It was only fair.

Her left eyebrow rose. "How 'bout I show you?"

With her hands on my arms, she backed me up to the sofa in my office.

The one where all my visitors sat.

When I reached it, I lowered myself to sitting, and Cricket, with her newfound ballsy confidence, lifted one leg on either side of my thighs, and straddled my lap.

That's what I'm talking about.

I grabbed a fistful of her plush ass with each hand, pulling her until her dress slid up and I could dry hump her lace-covered pussy. The heat she was pouring on my cock was nearly unbearable, so I reached between her legs, slipped my fingers inside the crotch of her panties, and yanked until they ripped. My girl was spread, exposed, and ready.

She gasped, the violence of the tearing fabric startling her. Our lips crashed together again, and I slid my fingers along her slit until my hand was soaked. Slipping a finger inside her, I made a *come here* motion that had her moaning against my mouth.

"Come on me, baby," I urged.

But before she did, she reached down and through a tangle of shirt tails, boxer shorts, and jeans, she got her hands on my cock. She entwined her fingers around my hard-on and began to stroke.

While she did, I reached into my back pocket. I tore open a condom and slid it down my erection after moving her hands out of the way.

When I was sheathed, I leaned back on the sofa and relaxed. I wanted to see my beautiful girl take control.

It was time for the Cricket show. And she did not disappoint.

She pushed aside her tattered panties and raised herself, so the tip of my cock stood at her entrance. Rubbing her clit, she lowered herself onto my sensitive head.

She stopped before going too far and swiveled her hips just enough to tease me. It was all I could do to resist grabbing her hips and slamming her down on my dick until I was inside her up to my aching balls.

I could be patient. To a point.

With her hands on my shoulders, she rocked her hips and took more of me, eventually engulfing my entire cock.

As tempted as I was to grab her tits for leverage, I let her run the show.

And run the show, she did.

Head rearing, her moans grew until her pussy clenched my cock. She went silent, shuddering from head to toe as a pink tinge washed across her chest and neck.

Just as her head fell limp onto my shoulder, I moved my hands to encircle her waist, where I pulled her down on my cock and held her until I exploded seconds later.

"Fuck. baby, you're incredible."

We sat like that for I don't know how long, catching our breath. I couldn't remember the last time I was so relaxed.

I helped her off me and lay her down on the sofa with her head on my lap. Stroking her hair, I held her hand with my other.

She sighed deeply.

"You good?" I asked.

"Mmmm. God yes." She pushed herself up to sitting and looked at me.

"I have a proposition for you," she said.

I tried not to laugh. "And what would that be?"

"It involves a weekend away. With me."

CHAPTER 21

CRICKET

I was doing my best to hide my excitement. Not sure I was succeeding.

"I have to hand it to you, Cricket, your story about Senator Richardson was solid. I mean, it was a fresh take on the *new guy in town* story. It's not easy to do that."

"Thank you, Ken, and thank you for the opportunity."

He held his hands up. "No, all thanks go to you. It was because of your connection, and persistence, that we got the first interview with Richardson."

Um, yeah...

"Do you think you'd like to try more news stories? We can have you cover general topics for now and then specialize later. What do you think?"

What did I think? Was he fucking kidding me?

"That'd be great, Ken," I said breezily. "Will Wayne be on board? I hate to leave him high and dry."

Not.

Ken shook his head. "Don't worry about Wayne. I'll take care of him."

I'm sure he would.

Once back at my desk, I looked around the disaster that was my cube. Surely with new responsibility at the paper, I'd get better digs, right?

Right?

"Cricket."

Fuck, I hated when people sneaked up behind me.

"Oh, hi, Wayne."

He looked confused. "You're leaving obits?"

How did he already know? And were his feelings hurt? Because it sure sounded like it.

"Um, eventually. Just talked to Ken about it."

"I thought you like obits. You know, honoring the dead and such."

This was how a man who enjoyed going to funerals viewed the world.

"I do like it, Wayne. Very much. I'll miss it."

That was a whopper of a lie.

"But I hope we can collaborate from time to time," I continued.

He smiled, relieved I wasn't totally abandoning him.

"Hey, I just heard the news," Aimee said as she barged into my cube.

Wayne looked at her like she was the enemy and slunk off.

She watched him go. "I take it he's not very happy?" she whispered.

I craned my neck to make sure he was out of earshot. "He's never happy, are you kidding? He likes *funerals*, for heaven's sake."

"Well, I just want to say congrats. It couldn't have happened to a nicer person. I knew you'd get your big break eventually."

The lump in my throat that I'd been fighting for an hour suddenly got bigger. And I didn't care.

My eyes filled, and one big fat tear ran down my cheek. "Thank you, Aimee. You've been a good friend."

I popped out of my chair and hugged her tightly.

"Okay, no more crying. I'm getting some people together, and we'll go celebrate after work, okay?"

"Really? Oh, thank you."

I never thought anyone in the office would want to celebrate anything about me. But I guess I'd proven myself, one way or the other.

It felt good.

No, actually, it felt great.

My future at the paper wasn't a sure thing by any stretch of the imagination. I'd have to keep proving myself every day. But I was one step closer to my goal and a big step further from falling on my ass.

My ambitions weren't too big. I was worthy of them, and they were worthy of me.

"Hi, Mom."

This was going to be interesting.

"Cricket, how are you?" she asked.

"Good, Mom. Hey, I have some news for you."

Drum roll...

"I'm getting some new responsibilities at the paper. I'm going to work on news now."

She gasped. "Oh, honey, that's great. I knew you could do it. That's so incredible..."

Really?

"But Mom, you're always bugging me to move back and work for a local paper. As if you never believed I could make it in D.C."

"Oh, Cricket, you've got that wrong. I've always believed in you. I was hard on you because I knew you could do great things. And you have. I know the girls' car accident way back when impacted you deeply. You were never the same after it."

Okay, now the tears were flowing. Again.

"Even though you hadn't been in that car that night, a little piece of you died, too. The only way you'd survive was if you got away. I knew that, sweetie. I wanted you to know you'd always have a life here if you wanted it, but I also knew you were destined for other things."

Well I'd be damned.

"Oh, Mom, I had no idea. Thank you. It means so much to hear that."

"You're welcome, sweetie. Now, when will I see your first story?"

I settled into the divey Irish bar near the office with all my coworkers for a celebratory beer. Even my bitchy coworker Sadie had joined us.

She leaned into the center of the table so everyone could hear her. "Don't look now, but the youngest, hottest senator ever just walked in."

A wave of heat washed over me as I turned in the same direction everyone else at the table did.

But Talbot's gaze immediately found mine, and he didn't even notice the other folks sitting with me.

"Hey, baby," he said, leaning down to kiss my cheek. He pulled over an empty chair from the table next to us and joined the party.

To say that most of the people at the table, especially Sadie, were shocked, was an understatement. Conversation came to a stop, and several beers halted mid-air.

Someone even gasped.

But Aimee more than made up for them, normalizing a not-very-normal situation. "Senator, so glad you could come. I knew Cricket would love the surprise."

"Aimee, call me Talbot. Or Tal. Not Senator. By this time of day, I'm tired of that shit."

Laughter exploded around the table.

"Thanks for having me," he said, raising a beer to the crowd. "And congrats to Cricket. Good times lie ahead for our girl."

Cheers rang out all around me.

When did I become one of the lucky ones?

Saltwater wind blasted my face, and I pulled my fleece tighter about me and my wool hat down to my eyes. We stood at the rear of the Block Island Ferry where, for the entire fifty-five minute ride, Talbot kept his arms around me to ward off the chill. I snuggled my cold nose against his neck and inhaled his simple, clean scent.

Just how I liked it.

Sure, we could have gone inside the ferry's cabin and hung out with the rest of the gang heading to the weekend house Bridget and Simon had rented, but we wanted some time to ourselves. The gathering promised to be a blast, but it wouldn't exactly be quiet and romantic. There would be time for that later.

Not that we'd been deprived. Just the weekend before, we'd escaped to Talbot's Manhattan loft for a couple days of Netflix and Chinese delivery. I couldn't even tell you what the weather outside had been. Rain?

Sun? No idea. We were completely immersed in each other. I didn't want to leave and return to reality.

We'd even had brunch with his parents again. I don't know if he'd had a talk with them or not, but they sure were a little warmer to me than they had been last time.

A little warmer. Not a lot.

We hadn't flown to New York for that trip. Instead, we'd taken Talbot's car.

We didn't want to take our new puppy on a plane just yet. We figured the car would be less stressful for him.

Yup, Talbot had gotten me a puppy. He'd gone to the DogHouse and asked them to find out which little pup I'd bonded with the best, and he brought that one home. Well, to *his* home, since I couldn't have pets in my apartment.

As the bluffs of Block Island came into view, the puppy whined from between Talbot's feet. He picked him right up and he three of us huddled together.

"We're gonna spoil this little bugger, but I can't help it," I said.

I put my face up close to him, and he licked me before I could jump back.

"We really need to come up with a name for him. It's been two weeks," I said.

Talbot shrugged. "I told you, he's your pup, and you have to name him. Throw caution to the wind. Just name him the first thing that comes to mind."

I burrowed my face in Talbot's delicious shoulder and inhaled his scent—plain soap and manly man.

He bent to kiss me, and I hoped his kisses would always be as exciting as they were that day. I knew they would.

Of course, there were lots of other things I didn't know besides what to call my new puppy.

But with Talbot at my side, and a puppy of my own, I knew I'd be able to figure out most anything life threw our way.

Like deals and other cool stuff? Sign up for the Mika Lane newsletter!

EPILOGUE

Talbot

What happened to Carlotti, that cocksucker who'd tried to ruin me? He was sued in civil court and made to pay restitution, which I donated to both the community center basketball program, and my other favorite charity, DogHouse. Anderson Cooper covered the story from soup to nuts, and let's just say—no one from the Carlotti family would be running for office ever again.

I managed to wrestle the puppy mill bill from Cazzo, who never cared about it anyway. The distinguished senator, by the way, abruptly decided to retire when his wife left him for a younger man. He retreated from his 'society' world, and my parents hadn't heard from him since.

My horndog chief of staff, Bruce, met Cricket's work buddy, Aimee. They were madly in lust, and I had to threaten him regularly not to have sex in my office.

My dear friend Halliday Hayes gave up on her powerful older men thing and started dating a limo driver. Apparently they had hot sex in every parking garage in D.C.

And the puppy?

Cricket named him Slick.

COCKY HERO CLUB

Want to keep up with all of the new releases in Vi Keeland and Penelope Ward's Cocky Hero Club world? Make sure you sign up for the official Cocky Hero Club newsletter for all the latest on our upcoming books: https://www.subscribepage.com/CockyHeroClub Check out other books in the Cocky Hero Club series: http://www.cockyheroclub.com

OTHER BOOKS BY MIKA LANE

The Anti-Hero Chronicles
Dirty Game / Audio
Nasty Bet / Audio
Filthy Deal / Audio
Foolish Dare / Audio

The Savage Mountain
Men Reverse Harem Series
The Captive / Audio
The Runaway / Audio
The Pursued / Audio
The Prize / Audio
Boxset books 1-4 / Audio

Contemporary Reverse Harem
The Inheritance / Audio
The Renovation / Audio

The Promotion / Audio
The Gallery / Audio
The Collection / Audio
Boxset books 1-5

A Player Romance series 1-3
Mister Hollywood
Mister Fake Date
Mister Wrong

Billionaire Duet 1-2
Dirty Little Secret
Sinful Little Betrayal

KEEP IN TOUCH

* * *

STAY IN THE KNOW
Join my Insider Group
Exclusive access to private release specials, giveaways, the opportunity to receive advance reader copies (ARCs), and other random musings.

LET'S KEEP IN TOUCH
Mika Lane Newsletter
Email me
Visit me! www.mikalane.com
Friend me! Facebook
Pin me! Pinterest
Follow me! Twitter
Laugh with me! Instagram

ABOUT THE AUTHOR

Dear Reader:

Please join my Insider Group and be the first to hear about giveaways, sales, pre-orders, ARCs, and other cool stuff: http://mikalane.com/join-mailing-list.

Writing has been a passion of mine since, well, forever (my first book was "The Day I Ate the Milky-way," a true fourth-grade masterpiece). These days, steamy romance, both dark and funny, gives purpose to my days and nights as I create worlds and characters who defy the imagination. I live in magical Northern California with my own handsome alpha dude, sometimes known as Mr. Mika Lane, and an evil cat named Bill. These two males also defy my imagination from time to time.

A lover of shiny things, I've been known to try to new recipes on unsuspecting friends, find hiding places so I can read undisturbed, and spend my last dollar on a plane ticket somewhere.

I have several titles for you to choose from including the perennially favorite Billionaire and Reverse Harem stories. And have you see my Player Series about male escorts who make the ladies of Hollywood curl their toes and forget their names? Hottttt.... And my brand new anti-hero/mafia books are coming out in audio as I write this.

Exciting news: in June 2020, I will be publishing with Vi Keeland's and Penelope Ward's Cocky Hero Club as one of their contributing authors. Stay tuned for more on this or follow my Facebook page: https://www.facebook.com/mikalaneauthor. And, as if that's not cool enough, I am also writing in K. Bromberg's Everyday Heroes world. Look for that later in the year.

I'll always promise you a hot, sexy romp with kick-ass but imperfect heroines, and some version of a modern-day happily ever after.

I LOVE to hear from readers when I'm not dreaming up naughty tales to share. Join my Insider Group so we can get to know each other better http://mikalane.com/join-mailing-list, or contact me here: https://mikalane.com/contact.

xoxo

Love,

Mika

Made in the USA
Monee, IL
22 June 2020